MARRY ME

DELANEY DIAMOND

GARDEN AVENUE PRESS

1

"**M**an, I can't thank you enough." Another satisfied customer.

Reginald smiled as he listened to the man sing his praises about the party Reginald and his small firm, Divorce Party Consultants, planned and executed for him last night.

As a divorce party consultant, Reginald was more than a coordinator for the party. He and his staff were counselors and cheerleaders. Some of these men were down bad. The divorces left them either with crushed egos, broken hearts, anger issues, or a combination of all three. Knowing he could provide a respite from the darkness made his work worthwhile.

"You're welcome, man. I'm glad you enjoyed yourself."

"I sure did. The dancers were a nice touch. I didn't expect them."

Reginald chuckled. The dancers didn't work for every client, but in the ten years he had been doing this work, he'd become a very good judge of character and recognized which clients could handle which type of parties. More importantly, which clients could handle the unique surprises they planned in order to make the event extra special.

"Listen, I gotta run, but you should be receiving a survey later today. Do me a favor and fill it out. Let us know what we did right, and let us know what we can improve on. We want to provide the best service to all our clients. We want them all to be happy, like you are."

"I can tell you right now, there's nothing I would change. Five stars across the board."

"That's what I like to hear. Have a good day."

"You too."

Reginald hung up, tugging his jacket a little closer. The February air carried a bit of chill in the early morning, but in typical fashion, by midday the weather would be warm enough for him to remove the jacket and enjoy the sunshine.

His eyes snagged on a woman crossing the street wearing a yellow peacoat and a gold and blue scarf. Head bent, she was busy texting. He couldn't see her whole face, but something about her was vaguely familiar.

Does she live or work around here? he wondered. Maybe that's why she seemed familiar to him.

As he was about to turn away, a taxi came rolling down the street, and he paused. The woman hadn't looked up from her phone, and he watched with alarm as she stepped off the sidewalk, still distracted by the device in her hand.

"Hey," he said, trying to get her attention.

His head swiveled toward the coming car. The driver wasn't paying attention either because he was also texting.

Holy smokes, he was going to hit her!

"Hey!" Reginald said, louder this time to get her attention.

The woman stopped in the middle of the road and followed his line of sight. When she saw the vehicle, her eyes widened, and she froze.

Reginald dashed between the cars and knocked her off her

feet. He took the brunt of the blow by twisting his body beneath hers before they hit the ground.

The sound of tires grating on the pavement greeted his ears as he gazed up at the woman on top of him.

She pressed her hands against his chest, her hips glued to his, and warmth invaded his loins.

Now that they were eye to eye, he knew exactly who she was, and the dawn of acknowledgement entered her eyes too.

"Lorna!" he said at the same time she said, "Reggie?"

They stared at each other in shock.

Then she started laughing. "Are you okay?"

Reginald shifted and pain arrowed through his lower back. He grimaced. "I'll live."

The driver, a middle-aged man with dark hair, raced over to them. "Are you okay?" he asked, eyes wide.

Lorna pushed to her feet and Reginald gingerly followed suit.

"You need to watch where you're going," he said, his voice icy with anger as he dusted off his pants.

"I'm sorry. I didn't see her."

"Because you were looking at your phone."

Shamefaced, the man nodded his head vigorously.

"I wasn't paying attention either," Lorna said.

"But he could've run you over. You would have been seriously hurt, possibly dead," Reginald pointed out.

The driver backed away from them. "I'll be much more careful from now on."

"You're not supposed to be texting and driving," Reginald called after him. "That's illegal."

The man must have taken the statement as a threat, because he made a run for the car, hopped in, and drove away.

"Well, I'm fine, thanks to you," Lorna said.

"You're taking this near death experience way better than you should." Granted, she should have been paying attention too, but the person behind the wheel held a greater obligation for safety.

"Are you guys okay?" A woman with her hands on a stroller called out to them from across the street.

"We're fine." Reginald dusted off his jacket sleeves.

"I guess you saved my life," Lorna said.

"I wouldn't say all that. He wasn't going fast."

"Well, like you pointed out, at the very least, I could have been badly injured." She cocked her head to the side. "How have you been?"

"Okay. It's been awhile."

"About fifteen or sixteen years, right?"

"Something like that," Reginald said.

They met sophomore year in biology class. Despite the size of the huge lecture hall, he noticed her right away, sitting up front, taking copious notes.

She hadn't changed much. She'd put on a little weight, her body more curvaceous than their college days, but she practically looked like she could be in college now. With tennis shoes on her feet, she wore an oversized sweater and black leggings. Her hair was much shorter than back in their university days. Back then, it had been long enough for a ponytail. Now, it was a short pixie brushed to one side of her attractive face. She wore minimal makeup, except for a rich red color on her plump lips. Her bright, amber-colored skin reminded him of the petals of a sunflower.

"So what's been up with you? I remember you were dating Byron. He lived across the hall from me. You two still together?"

"No, that ended pretty soon after college. He moved to Arizona for grad school, and last I heard, he's married with kids now."

"And you're not married?"

A shadow passed over her features, and he wondered what caused the sudden change in her otherwise sunny disposition.

Then she shook her head. "Nope. And you? Still a ladies' man?"

Reginald took a step back and clutched his chest. "Whoa, a ladies' man? Come on now, where did you hear that?"

"I heard some things. Plus Byron told me all about your many ladies."

That son of a... "He did, did he?"

"Mhmm."

"Forget everything he said. I was a nice guy and still am. I was friendly, that's all."

"Is that right?" She raised a skeptical eyebrow.

"That's right."

"But you're not married?"

"No."

"Ever come close?" she asked.

"No," Reginald admitted.

"Too busy enjoying yourself, I guess."

"There you go again."

She smiled.

They faced each other for several seconds until the moment became awkward. Reginald didn't want to leave but couldn't think of a reason to stick around and continue talking.

"I was on my way to get coffee at the shop up the street. Never thought I'd almost die getting my morning treat."

She laughed—a light, delightful sound that made his scalp tingle.

"Would you like to join me for a cup of coffee?" she asked.

Temptation made him hesitate, but then his head cleared. "Can't. I have a meeting I need to get to in ten minutes. But maybe we could grab coffee another time."

"I'd like that. We could—Hey, I just thought of something."

"What?"

"Didn't you have a nickname back in school?"

"Nah. Don't know what you're talking about," Reginald lied.

"Yes. They used to call you something..." Lorna narrowed her eyes as she tried to remember.

"You might have me mistaken with someone else," Reginald said.

Her eyes widened as the memory came back, and he inwardly groaned.

"The Green-Eyed Bandit! Because you stole so many hearts."

"Don't remind me," he muttered.

"You're not ashamed of your past, are you?"

"I'm not ashamed, but I'd rather not go back down that road, if you don't mind. Now, about that coffee...."

"I don't know if I should risk it. You might steal my heart."

He knew when a woman was flirting, and she was definitely flirting. Her eyes were bright, and her voice had dropped lower and turned a little sultry. He was feeling her, so it was nice to see her feeling him too.

"I don't steal hearts, but I do think that since I did kind of save your life, you owe me. I don't know if coffee will cover it."

"Oh?" She crossed her arms over her chest.

He flung up his hands in defense. "Hold on, I'm not suggesting anything sinister. Just dinner. That's not unreasonable, is it?"

Studying her in the cool morning air, the softness in her eyes and the half smile on her lips indicated she was more interested in him than she probably wanted to let on. He certainly wouldn't mind hooking up. She was attractive and had animated, friendly brown eyes and a pair of lips he suddenly ached to kiss.

He didn't see her much on campus after they didn't have biology class together anymore. Time had temporarily erased her from his memory. He sowed his wild oats, and her relationship with Byron made her off limits. But maybe he could make up for lost time.

"I guess dinner isn't unreasonable," she agreed.

Her face broke into a brilliant smile. Wow. His lower abs tightened as awareness rippled through his body.

"Cool. Give me your phone, and I'll add my number to it."

She did as he asked, and afterward she called his number so he could have her information.

"Are you free Saturday night?" Lorna asked.

"Saturday night is perfect," Reginald said.

"I'll call you when everything is set."

"I'll be waiting."

An impish smile crossed her face. "Bye, Reggie."

"Bye, Lorna."

He watched her walk away before heading down the sidewalk to his appointment. Luckily, he had arrived a little early, so despite this slight interruption, he would still make the meeting on time.

Before he entered the building, he shot a last minute glance in the direction Lorna had taken. She stopped as she opened the door to the coffee shop and waved at him before slipping inside.

2

Lorna walked up to the Crosby Nuptials building, holding a cup tray with four coffees.

The facility contained event space on one side and offices on the other. She entered through the office door and flashed a smile at the receptionist flipping through a bridal magazine. Drea wore glasses and her hair in an Afro puff on top of her head.

Her eyes widened with joy when she saw the coffee Lorna carried. She stretched across the desk with both hands, palms up. "Gimme."

Lorna held the cups away from her. "Who said one of these is for you?"

"You wouldn't be so cruel as to taunt me," Drea said with a whine.

Lorna laughed and placed one of the cups in her hand. "You have a problem."

"I know. I'll get help one of these days." Drea removed the cover and inhaled the steam, eyes closed, a euphoric expression on her face. Then she took a sip.

"Get help immediately," Lorna said as she walked away.

She delivered the second coffee to a male coordinator, one of the few people who came in early every day.

"Look at you, doing the Lord's work," he said.

"I don't do this for everybody. Just you," Lorna said with a grin.

He chuckled before returning his attention to the computer screen.

Lorna went down the quiet hallway to her boss's office. Tessa stood with her back to the door, rummaging through a drawer in her file cabinet. Her short natural hair was speckled with gray, her stout figure dressed in black slacks and a beige pullover sweater.

Lorna rapped her knuckles against the door frame and then waltzed into the office. "Good morning."

Tessa glanced over her shoulder, shooting a look at Lorna over her gold-framed glasses. "What has you so chipper?"

"Am I being chipper?"

"Yes. More than usual." Her boss pulled out a folder stuffed with invitation samples and slammed the drawer shut.

Lorna placed a coffee on the cluttered desk and dropped into the chair. "I had an interesting morning."

Tessa fisted a hand at her hip. "Tell me more."

Despite the thirty year age difference, they got along well because they were both romantics, and she believed Tessa saw herself as a mother figure to Lorna.

Lorna started working for her five years ago after leaving a position as an event planner at a hotel. After the tragic death of her fiancé, she had been looking for something new and distracting. When she saw the opening for a wedding planner, she applied and was hired, and immediately she and Tessa Crosby developed a rapport.

When Tessa decided to focus on the niche market of vow renewals, she put Lorna in charge of that aspect of the business.

For the past three years, they had seen double-digit growth in that area.

Last year they landed a high-profile vow renewal for former baseball player Damon "The Flash" Foster and his wife, Audra. The resulting PR catapulted the company's name and business took off, making them one of the top companies in the state. They were so busy, Lorna spent less time coordinating ceremonies and more of her time negotiating with vendors and helping Tessa build their clientele.

"I ran into someone from my past—an old college friend who rescued me, if you can believe that," Lorna said.

"Thanks for the coffee. Rescued you how?" Tessa sat at the desk.

Lorna told her how she had not been paying attention while texting, was almost run over, and finished by explaining she had plans to meet with Reginald Saturday night.

"You've had quite the morning. Glad you didn't get hurt. Now this man... he sounds promising. And with a name like Knight, that's a good omen, don't you think? Maybe your knight in shining armor has arrived." Tessa wiggled her eyebrows.

Lorna laughed. "I doubt it."

"I don't know, I see running into an old boyfriend from college as a positive sign."

"I said he's an old friend, not a *boy*friend."

"The way you described him, I thought... Are you not attracted to him?"

"I wouldn't say that," Lorna hedged.

She was downplaying her interest, but her immediate, pulse-thumping attraction couldn't be ignored. Reginald was a good-looking man with dark tawny skin and a clean-shaven face. She could stare into his arresting green eyes all day and imagined that his full lips would wreak havoc delivering delicious kisses all over her body.

"What would you say?" Tessa rested her chin on her fist, giving Lorna her undivided attention.

Sipping coffee, Lorna sat with her thoughts for a moment. "Being totally honest—yes, I am attracted to him, but Reggie and I were only friends in college. Matter of fact, the guy I dated throughout my years at UA was a friend of his. Reggie was never interested in settling down with one woman. He had a reputation on campus, if you know what I mean."

"That's a pretty big campus."

"But the number of Black students on campus was very small. If you were remotely popular, people knew you or knew of you. Plus, he joined a fraternity, which elevated his notoriety. He spent a lot of time with a lot of different women, and I spent all my time with my boyfriend, Byron. Eventually, our friendship fell off." Lorna shrugged as she brought the coffee cup to her lips.

"A man who is handsome and willing to risk bodily harm to protect you sounds like a keeper to me. If you're not interested in him, what's the purpose of meeting for dinner on Saturday night?"

"Like I said, as a thank you for saving my butt. I guess we'll catch up too."

Tessa's expression turned thoughtful. "Be careful," she warned.

Lorna laughed. "That sounds ominous."

"Because he sounds like the kind of man who can sweep you off your feet. You're looking for a real relationship, and he probably isn't."

"I don't know what he's looking for at this stage in life, but he is good-looking, seems to still have a good sense of humor, and wears nice-sized... shoes."

Tessa arched an eyebrow. "He has big feet?"

"Mhmm. By the size of them, I'd say he's blessed and highly favored." Lorna brought the cup to her lips again.

Tessa's head tossed back in laughter. "This is exactly what I'm talking about. You're interested in this man as more than a friend."

Lorna laughed. "I made an observation, that's all. I'm not going to get my emotions all tangled up. Besides, who's to say he's interested in me in that way? He probably sees me as only a friend, like he did back at UA. As for me, I know what I want, and it's not a fling with an old college friend."

Though, there was something about his eyes when he smiled. They held a warmth that invited her to know more, which was very tempting.

Tessa cradled her cup in both hands. "All right, Miss I'm-Not-Interested-In-A-Fling. Where are you taking him for dinner?"

"I'm not sure. I was trying to think of a restaurant where we could take our time, eat good food, and catch up."

Tessa fixed her mouth into a moue. Seconds later, her eyes brightened. "I know the perfect place, a little French restaurant in downtown Decatur called La Petite Maison. Bear and I used to eat there every so often. My husband was picky, but he loved their food. The restaurant is small and cozy, and after dinner you could go to the ice cream shop around the corner for dessert and walk around the square to chat some more."

"Ooh, excellent idea, and you can't go wrong with French food. Thanks for the tip. I'll get my butt to work now." Lorna stood but paused before leaving. "Don't you have a hot date this weekend?"

"I canceled it. I'm on hiatus."

"Again?"

"Yes. I ended up canceling after our last phone call went left. These men out here are hit or miss, chile. Don't be an old bird like me trying to date in your sixties. I'm seriously considering giving up. I don't know why I bother."

"You think you'll ever get married again?"

Tessa had been married for over twenty years before cancer took her husband. Right before he passed, they renewed their vows. That's how she'd gotten the idea to focus on vow renewal in the business. The ceremony had reminded her of her love for her husband and the celebration with family and friends had brought them a lot of joy before his passing.

When she attended the ceremony, Lorna could see the love between them. The glow of happiness as Tessa's husband waited in a wheelchair at the front of the venue for her couldn't be faked.

Tessa sighed. "I'd love to get married again, but at my age, the pickings are slim. The men are either married, too old, or playing games. My Bear was a unique man. I was lucky to have him for as long as I did." A sad smile touched her lips.

Lorna matched her smile with a sad one of her own. "We both got lucky for a time."

Their eyes met, and they silently commiserated over their grief. Tessa had lost her husband of over twenty years to a deadly disease. Lorna had lost her fiancé to violence.

"And on that note, I'm really leaving now so I can get to work."

On the way out, Tessa called her name, and she turned.

"You're a great catch. You'll find someone."

Lorna smiled. "So will you."

3

Friday night, Reginald entered Double Trouble. After a long day, he was looking forward to a few drinks and good conversation with his cousins.

The family-owned bar was a favorite hangout for them. All manner of sports were always on the televisions on the walls, and tonight was no different with the Hawks playing the Bucks. As he scanned the crowded establishment, shouts of dismay and cheers of joy erupted from the pool room near the back.

He spotted Chase over at the bar and made his way in that direction. "Hey, what's up?"

"Nothing much," Chase said, a Jamie Foxx look-alike with a full beard.

"You been here long?"

Chase shook his head and held up his beer. "Only long enough to drink half of this."

"Where's Xavier?" Reginald sat on the stool beside him.

"He's not here yet but sent a text that he should be here soon. I'll order a beer for when he arrives."

Dani, a bartender and one of the owners, came over. "What'll you have tonight?" she asked Reginald.

In the past, he would have made a remark and said he'd have her, but ever since she got married, he toned down the flirtations.

"Full Moon beer."

"Make that two. Xavier should be here soon," Chase said.

"Coming right up." She disappeared to enter the order.

Minutes later, they had the beers and Xavier strolled in. He was a giant of a man at six feet four. He had a close-cropped beard and facial features like the actor Henry Simmons, but with locs.

Reginald and his cousins were thirty-five years old and born only months apart. Their mothers were sisters, and because they were so close in age, they grew up together like brothers instead of cousins.

They used to do everything together. As the eldest by a few months, Reginald was the one always leading them on adventures. They went camping, went fishing, and rode their bikes on neighborhood adventures. They knew about each other's first kiss and each teenage heartbreak.

He and his cousins always had each other's back too. Any fool who picked a fight with one was picking a fight with all three, and when Reginald ran track in high school, his cousins were always there to cheer him on.

"What took you so long to get here?" he asked.

Chase chuckled. "Maybe it was a woman... finally." He pushed the beer in front of Xavier.

While Reginald and Chase laughed, Xavier ignored them and tilted the bottle to his lips.

Dani reappeared and placed her hands on her hips. "Everything okay over here?"

Reginald suspected she was up to something.

"Yeah, we're good," Chase answered.

"What did you three get into for Valentine's Day?"

"I knew it. Don't answer that. It's a trick question," Reginald said, taking a huge swallow of his beer.

Valentine's Day had come and gone a couple of weeks ago. If he'd had a woman in his life, he would have spoiled her. Instead, he spent the day and night working.

"It is not," Dani said, sounding indignant.

"Just because you're happily married now doesn't give you the right to pick on single folks."

"I'm not picking on you, but since you mentioned being single, I do think it's odd that three good-looking men like yourselves are still single."

"It's not safe out there for men. Women are dangerous. Breaking hearts and whatnot," Reginald explained.

He shot a fake smile at Dani, and she pursed her lips.

"I know plenty of women who are looking for good men, and when they think they've found him—boop—he turns out to be a frog in prince clothing," she said.

Reginald chuckled.

"What's so funny?" Dani asked.

"You're hilarious, because you'll never acknowledge all the drama women put men through. The ones complaining about frogs in prince clothing are probably hags in princess clothing."

His cousins laughed.

"Oh really?" Dani said.

"Yes, really. I see it every day with my divorce party clients. Women are part of the now culture. They want everything to be perfect right now, and if it's not, they don't stick around. They completely miss out on good men like us because they're too quick to move on to the next guy, and the next guy, and the next one."

"Sad but true," Chase said in a grim tone, the corners of his mouth curling upward in silent laughter.

"I didn't do anything on Valentine's Day, so I'm here to find my future wife," Xavier joked.

"I'm supposed to believe that you're looking for love?" Dani asked.

"Is that so hard to believe?" Reginald shot back in defense of his cousin.

Dani's eyes narrowed, and he braced for her words.

"You guys are idiots," she said, hands on her hips. "Reggie, you're too cynical to ever find love. Though deep down, I think you want to, but that career of yours says otherwise. Xavier, you're too busy building your trucking business and coaching teen basketball to find love, though you claim to be ready for marriage. And you," she narrowed her eyes at Chase, "need to quit leading these women on. You make them think they have a chance with you when it's clear you don't know what the hell you want."

"Oh no. We're not doing this tonight," Chase murmured under his breath. He grabbed his bottle from the bar and stood.

Reginald and Xavier followed. As they walked away, Reginald could hear Dani's mouth still going.

They searched for a table in the packed bar and spotted one near the back. Reginald and Xavier sat across from Chase, and a server came over and took their orders before leaving them alone.

Chase shook his head. "Dani is a trip. Ever since she got married, she's been trying to marry everyone off. And I think she calls us idiots at least once every few weeks."

"She wouldn't have said anything if Xavier hadn't joked about coming in here to find his future wife," Reginald said.

"Yeah, that's on me." Xavier gave them a sheepish grin. "The words came out of my mouth before I realized it. I hate that we have to be on guard when talking about women around her. *Especially* now that she's happily married."

"She was definitely on a roll tonight."

The conversation segued into other topics. Sports, politics, the weather, and, as usual—women.

They spent some time talking about Wynter's offer to make Chase a partner in her business. Unfortunately, his feelings for her were proving problematic. Reginald gave his usual no-nonsense advice, but they hardly listened to him regarding relationships anymore. Pulling rank as the oldest didn't work, either.

Xavier had a whole different issue with a woman he met tonight—Zena—the reason he was late meeting them. His cousin hadn't dated in a while because his last girlfriend turned into a stalker, so the fact that he didn't ask the woman for her number didn't surprise Reginald.

The candid conversations prompted him to share what happened between him and Lorna on Monday.

"Remember that girl I had a crush on back in college? Lorna? I ran into her on Monday."

"Was she the one in your biology class?" Chase asked.

"That's the one."

"I remember Lorna. You had it bad for her," Xavier said.

"I wouldn't say bad."

"Dawg, you were ready to turn in your player card until that guy—what was his name...?" Chase frowned, trying to remember.

"Byron," Reginald said, the name tasting bitter on his tongue.

"That's right. Byron asked her out, and they started dating. Wasn't there something shady about the whole thing? He knew you liked her, didn't he?"

"Yes, the bastard."

"That was grimy what he did. If I remember correctly, they stayed together all through college, didn't they?" Xavier asked.

"They did. I asked her about him. Turns out they didn't stay together after college. He moved away for graduate school and eventually the relationship fell apart. Anyway, you'll never believe how we ran into each other. She was crossing the street, not paying attention because she was looking at her phone. A taxi driver coming down the street was texting and driving and almost ran her over. I had to knock her out of the way."

"That's pretty dramatic," Chase said, taking a sip of beer.

"Is she okay?" Xavier asked.

"She's fine, but we're going out tomorrow night since she owes me for rescuing her. This is a friendly meal though."

"Friendly. Oh, okay." Chase tossed a skeptical glance in his direction.

"You're not funny," Reginald told him.

"You expect us to believe you're going to be friends with this woman? You used to be crazy about her."

Reginald laughed. "First of all, I wasn't crazy about her, and second, even if I was, things have changed."

"Are you saying you don't see her that way anymore?" Xavier asked.

"I mean... I still think she's cute. And sexy. And she seems to have the same sense of humor. But we're going out as friends, and that's all."

"Okay, cool. Two buddies hanging out. Platonically."

"Yes," Reginald said, laughing again. "Why did you say it like that?"

"Because you don't have female friends." Xavier shot a look at Chase, lifting his right eyebrow in a silent request for agreement.

"You really don't," Chase cosigned.

"Well, Lorna might be the first," Reginald said.

"Yeah right," Xavier said. "We know you, Reggie. The last thing on your mind is friendship. It's us. Admit that you're interested."

"All right, I'm interested! But you know me, I'm careful. She might end up being like one of those women who divorces my clients. Or she could end up being like you-know-who."

Xavier groaned. "Bria."

"That's the one."

Bria had been the closest Reginald had ever come to getting married. They started dating soon after he left the university and moved back to Atlanta. After several years together, she started pressuring him to get married. Though he'd considered it, he didn't think he was in good financial shape at that point because he was working a full-time job while trying to get Divorce Party Consultants off the ground.

His explanations weren't good enough. Bria was part of the "now" culture he'd complained to Dani about. She dumped him because he wasn't moving fast enough.

"I think we all know I dodged a bullet with her."

"True," Xavier nodded.

Chase's eyes were thoughtful as he looked at Reginald. "Does Lorna have any idea that you used to like her?"

"Not a clue," Reginald answered.

"Is it possible your feelings were—or are—reciprocated?"

A smile broke out on Reginald's face. "I'll find out tomorrow night."

4

S tanding outside the restaurant, Reginald checked his watch. He'd arrived a few minutes early because oddly enough, he'd been a little nervous and wanted to make a good impression. He was generally a confident person, but Lorna left him feeling unbalanced—and this wasn't even a date.

He had taken extra care with his appearance, buying a new shirt in pale yellow that went well with his charcoal slacks, shining his black shoes, and going to the barbershop for a haircut. He'd debated wearing cologne and at the last minute splashed on his favorite scent before bolting out the door.

Laughing a bit to himself, he had to admit that he was trying to impress her. Maybe his cousins were right. Maybe he did have it bad for her at one time.

Nah. He had liked her, and she was cool people, but his feelings for her hadn't been any stronger than they were for other women in his life around that time.

A few minutes later, Lorna sashayed down the sidewalk toward him, and he froze, watching her hip-swinging movements in nude heels and a long sweater with sleeves that came to her elbows. The open sweater revealed a figure-hugging taupe dress. She wore gold jewelry around her neck and in her ears, which brightened her effervescent, welcoming smile.

Hell, the sight of her damn near sucked the air from his lungs.

She stopped in front of him, her bright smile wavering. "Is something wrong?"

Reginald suddenly realized he hadn't smiled back because he'd been busy staring at her. He shook his head to clear the cobwebs.

"No, nothing's wrong. You look... spectacular. Matter of fact, I feel like I'm underdressed."

She laughed, the same engaging laugh he'd heard the other day. "You're fine. I attended an event that ran over and didn't have time to go home and change, so I came straight here."

"You should've told me. We could have postponed to another night."

"Oh no, absolutely not. Besides, I'm starving. Ready to go inside?"

"Sure." Reginald opened the door and let her in ahead of him.

The strong aroma of food with notes of rosemary and thyme, filled the air of the small restaurant. There were approximately twelve tables close together. On the walls hung pictures of the French countryside and Parisian attractions like the Eiffel Tower and the Arc de Triomphe. Signs and wooden placards with French words he didn't understand, and some he did, also decorated the walls.

A slender woman with frizzy, curly hair and no makeup approached them, wiping her hands on an apron tied around her waist.

"*Bonjour.* I am Marie. Two for dinner?" she asked in a thick French accent.

"Yes," Lorna replied.

Marie seated them against a wall at a two top before leaving them alone to decide about their meals.

"Have you ever eaten here before?" Reginald asked, flipping open the menu.

"First time. My boss recommended it. She and her husband used to eat here before he passed, and she vouched for the food."

"The only French food I think I've ever had is quiche. Didn't care for it."

Her eyes widened in dismay. "Oh no, would you rather go somewhere else?"

"Not at all. I'm just letting you know I don't know much about French food, so you might have to guide me."

She grinned. "Not a problem. Matter of fact, why don't you let me order?"

Reginald sat back and gazed across the table at her. "I've never had a woman order for me before, but I guess I can give it a shot this time."

"I promise, you're in good hands."

Was that a flirty look she cast in his direction? Her expression suggested more than taking care of his ordering needs, and desire jabbed him in the stomach. If he didn't totally screw this up tonight, he might get lucky.

Perfect timing, considering his last hook up had been over a month ago. He'd been so busy with work he hadn't been concerned about not having sex. But seated across from Lorna, sex was definitely uppermost in his mind.

"Are you in the mood for meat or seafood?" she asked.

"Let's go with meat."

"I know the perfect dish for you."

Marie returned to the table and took their orders. Lorna ordered them both French onion soup to start. For herself, she chose the pan-roasted salmon with risotto and arugula. For him, she selected braised beef on a bed of tortellini with a tomato confit. He couldn't wait to try the dish.

There were only two people working in the dining room— Marie and a young woman. They both looked tired, so Reginald figured they were probably short-staffed, and he would need to be patient with the speed at which food came out of the kitchen.

"So, what have you been up to? I want to know everything," Reginald said.

"Everything?" She arched an eyebrow.

"Give me the condensed version," he amended with a laugh.

"Okay, let's see... after college, I and a friend moved to Atlanta. We were roommates until she found a job as a consultant and wanted her own place. Then we split up. I lucked out and found a cheap apartment and continued working in the hotel industry as an event coordinator."

"You liked it?"

"I did, for a while. Then a personal tragedy made me rethink what I was doing with my life. I became antsy and started looking for a change. That's when I found a job as a wedding coordinator. Specifically, I handle vow renewals."

Reginald wanted to ask about the personal tragedy, but the way she skipped over the topic made him think she wasn't inclined to go into further detail.

"Is vow renewals a big business?" he asked instead.

"It is. Most people think wedding coordination is restricted to people who are going to get married, but a growing number of couples are having ceremonies where they re-dedicate themselves to their marriage. Used to be, they were done during milestone anniversaries, such as the tenth or the twentieth anniversary, but nowadays people are doing them for all kinds of reasons. After they have kids, after a difficult period in their marriage, et cetera."

"Interesting."

"It's a lot of fun. In our job, we make people happy, and the romantic in me gets that little hit of adrenaline. Unfortunately, I don't coordinate as much as I'd like to anymore."

When she said "hit of adrenaline," a spark entered her eyes.

"Why not?"

"We've grown so much, nowadays I spend a lot of my time negotiating contracts, finding new clients, and getting in touch with old ones so we stay uppermost in their mind. Regular contact means they'll remember us when the next anniversary rolls around or they have a friend who's interested in doing the same thing. What about you? What have you been up to?"

"Like you, I moved here after I graduated. I worked in the restaurant industry for a while, and I almost got engaged."

Her eyes widened.

"Don't look so surprised."

She let out a little laugh. "I'm not. Okay, maybe I'm a little surprised."

"Because you never figured me for the settling down type?"

"I guess," she said carefully, cautiously, as if concerned about offending him. "But what do you mean, you almost got engaged?"

Before he could answer, Marie approached with two glasses of water and two glasses of wine on a tray—white for Lorna and red for him. The other server immediately approached with the French onion soup in clay cups.

"Mmm, this smells good. Thank you," Lorna said.

When the women left the table, he and Lorna tasted the soup.

"This is delicious," Reginald said.

She nodded her head in agreement. "Okay, you were about to tell me about your almost engagement, which I still can't believe."

"There's not much to tell. Our relationship was good for a

while, but she put a lot of pressure on me, and it eventually didn't work out."

"Maybe that's for the best."

"I agree. Matter of fact, I see better days ahead already." He held her gaze so there would be no misunderstanding what he meant.

Her cheeks reddened and dipping her eyes to the soup, she ate another spoonful.

Yeah, she got the message.

"After my breakup, I started organizing divorce parties full time."

Her eyebrows raised in surprise. "Excuse me?"

Reginald chuckled. "You heard me. My work is practically the opposite of yours. I organize divorce parties. Most of my clients are men looking to celebrate their freedom or forget their pain."

"How in the world did you get into that?"

"It happened by accident, to be honest. I used to be the manager for a restaurant. My dream was to one day become the area manager for all the locations, but a friend of mine got a divorce, and he was a mess. Barely eating, depressed for weeks, that kind of thing. I and a few of our buddies decided to throw him a party to shake him out of his funk. I did most of the work, and at the end of the night, a couple of the guys said I should plan more parties."

"That planted the seed." Lorna sipped her water.

Reginald nodded. "I did my research and started planning parties on the side. Next thing I know, the divorce parties income exceeded my manager's income. I quit my restaurant job. It was a no-brainer. Started ten years ago and been full-time for the past nine. Never looked back."

"Good for you. So I take it there's a big demand for your parties?"

"When I started the company, there wasn't much demand

for our services, and we used to plan parties for men and women. But the market has grown, with more companies organizing these parties. I concentrated on the men because, quite frankly, there wasn't really much of an outlet for men who were left in shambles after their wives left. A lot of these guys had half their money gone and no longer lived under the same roof as their kids—pretty traumatic, by the way. They struggled, in general. I like to think that having this party is a mental health boost for them. Like you, I get a little hit of adrenaline making them happy." He grinned.

"I guess we both make people happy, but in different ways."

"Exactly."

They continued talking, and the time passed quickly. She was easy to talk to. When the food arrived, Reginald cut into the meat and placed a morsel in his mouth. It was so tender it practically melted on his tongue. He let out a quick moan.

Her eyes brightened as she smiled. "Good?"

"Hella good."

They locked eyes for a moment, and he saw nothing but warmth and interest.

If he was reading her right—and he was good at reading women—they were definitely getting horizontal tonight.

5

There were only two customers inside the ice cream shop around the corner. Not surprising since the temperature hadn't increased enough to warrant an influx of people.

"I'm paying for the ice cream."

Behind her, Reginald had dipped his head close to whisper the words. A tingle raced up Lorna's spine when his breath brushed her ear.

She glanced back at him. "Dinner is on me, and dessert is part of dinner, which means I'm paying for the ice cream."

He shook his head. "No, I insist."

"Is that some macho thing that doesn't allow you to let me pay for everything?"

He laughed.

Ugh, he was so handsome. The whole time at dinner she kept wondering what it would be like to kiss him. How much deeper did his voice get when he rolled over in the morning and said *Good morning*?

"Call it whatever you want, but I'm uncomfortable allowing a woman to pay for everything on our date."

"We're not on a date," she reminded him.

His lips twisted into a sideways smirk. "You really believe that?"

Lorna let out a little laugh. "You are being mighty presumptuous, Reggie."

He laughed softly, his eyes lifting to the menu of choices on the wall behind the counter. "I'm not arguing with you. Pick your ice cream, and I'll pay."

Though she had no problem covering the cost of the ice cream, she appreciated his insistence on splitting the cost. When their turn came, they peered at the choices behind the glass. After a few taste tests, Lorna opted for a scoop of chocolate chip and a scoop of chocolate with brownie chunks. Reginald settled on two scoops of vanilla.

They exited the shop into the cool night air and strolled toward the center of the square. With spring around the corner, more people were out and about, taking advantage of the chance to be in the fresh outdoors, strolling from one location to the next—enjoying the coffee shops, bars, and restaurants in the area.

Lorna eyed Reginald's ice cream selection. "Vanilla?"

"I go with what I know."

"I never figured you for the playing-it-safe type," she said as they strolled side by side.

Ever the gentleman, he walked on the outside of the sidewalk, closest to the traffic. Whoever his momma was, she raised him right.

"Playing it safe sounds lame. I like to think I'm a careful person who evaluates every decision before making a choice. When you choose based on emotion rather than logic, that's when bad shit happens."

Lorna spooned ice cream into her mouth. "Are we talking about ice cream, or...?"

"Ice cream and life in general."

"There's a story there, I can tell."

"I'm just observant. The world ain't as nice as we would like it to be. Better safe than sorry."

They strolled in silence for a bit before she spoke again.

"I think you've been jaded by the work you do. You don't trust women, do you?"

He chuckled. "You're jumping to conclusions."

"I'm observant too. I listened to what you said at dinner."

He slanted a sideways glance at her as he spooned ice cream into his mouth. "Let me guess. You think love is ever-lasting."

"It can be," Lorna said with a shrug. "But not always. Byron and I didn't last, though at the time I thought I was in love with him. It hurt when he moved away, and it hurt when we broke up. But that's life. If you don't take swings, how do you know if you'll hit a home run?"

"Nice baseball analogy."

"Thank you," she said, blushing.

"I'm guessing you believe there's one person out there for all of us?"

"I'll put it this way. I believe we can find someone to spend our lives with, who makes us happy. Someone who we can get through the bad times with."

Reginald laughed, shaking his head.

Lorna stopped walking. "What is so funny?"

He faced her, his lips tilted upward in soft amusement. "You. You're one of *those* people."

"Excuse me?" she said, slightly offended.

"Don't get mad," Reginald said in a placating voice. "Your point of view is unrealistic, that's all. Those types of relation-ships don't exist, where everything is hunky dory and when problems arise, you work them out together. That's not real life. In real life, people are selfish. They do what's in their own best interest—not what's in the best interest of their relationship."

"Please tell me you're not serious."

"I'm absolutely serious."

Lorna ate her ice cream in silence. The more she listened to him talk, the more his cynicism concerned her.

"What's that frown for?" Reginald asked.

"I didn't realize I was frowning."

"You are. Because you don't like what I said."

"I think it's sad, that's all." She shrugged one shoulder.

"What's sad?"

"That you're so jaded. Who hurt you?"

Reginald snorted as if she'd said something absolutely ridiculous. "Nobody hurt me."

"Somebody hurt you," Lorna insisted.

"Okay fine, there is something from my past, but it's not a big deal. I was... kind of in love once before."

"Kind of in love? Is that like being kind of pregnant?"

"You have a smart mouth, you know that?"

"Sorry," she said, not sounding sorry at all. "Please continue."

"Anyway, remember I told you about my almost engagement? Well, I did want to get married. Bria—that's my ex's name—and I talked about getting married, how many kids we wanted, all that. But I was busy working at the restaurant and growing the divorce party business. I didn't have time to devote to her like I wanted, and I fully acknowledge that. But she was impatient. She couldn't understand that the timing was wrong. I couldn't work two jobs and get married and start a family. I needed a little more time."

"Which she wouldn't give you," Lorna guessed.

"No." That one word came out low and bitter. "She claimed her biological clock was ticking. By the way, we were only twenty-five at the time. She started constantly complaining about everything. She harassed me about kids. She wanted to know where our relationship was going. The worst was when she nagged me about working too much and gave me an ultimatum. I don't do well with ultimatums. I told her what I could do at the time, and she wasn't with that. During our last argument, we both said things we shouldn't have. After that, she moved out. That wasn't the way I wanted our relationship to end. Matter of fact, I didn't want it to end at all."

"I'm sorry that happened, but not all women are like that."

"Based on my experience, a lot of women are like that."

"Some people are worried about life leaving them behind. They want to live in the moment," Lorna said. She didn't know Bria, but that's what made the most sense in her mind.

"Yeah, well, impatience can cause you have to have regrets. I planned a party last week for a man whose wife left him because he didn't have enough ambition." Reginald shook his head. "She didn't think he was assertive enough, but it simply wasn't his time yet. Weeks after the divorce was final, he received a promotion he'd been working on for a while. Then you know what happened? She started calling him, trying to get back together. Smart man that he is, he resisted her and threw himself a divorce party. That one was nice. We rented a yacht in Miami, and a bunch of his friends flew down. We hired ladies for entertainment, and the men all had a blast."

If his smile was any indication, that must have been quite a party. Lorna could only imagine the shenanigans on a yacht in Miami with 'ladies for entertainment.'

"What matters is that he's happy now, but surely you don't believe women are the only ones causing relationships to end? For every story you tell me about a woman being the problem in the relationship, I have three about how problematic men can be. Unlike you, I'm not jaded. Love is... great. You should jump in with both feet when you find the right person."

"You need to take off those rose-colored glasses," Reginald said dryly.

Sheesh. This conversation was drying out her panties.

She'd considered sleeping with him tonight, but now she wasn't so sure. He might be her worst nightmare—a misogynistic jerk.

"Check out the couple up ahead," Reginald said in a lowered voice.

A man and women were standing near a bench and engaged in a heated argument. The woman yelled at the man while he stood with his hands stuffed in his coat pockets, glaring down at her. Every time he opened his mouth and tried to speak, she yelled louder and cut him off.

"Chances are, they're going to split up. Do you know why? Because she doesn't want to put in the work to make the relationship work. Poor guy can't get a word in edgewise." Reginald shook his head.

As they drew nearer, the woman took off, and the man lumbered after her.

"Poor bastard. If they're married, he'll be hiring my service soon enough to deal with his messy divorce after that obviously toxic relationship ends and she takes half his stuff."

A bit tired of hearing him bash women, Lorna said, "If they're a married couple, it's only fair that she gets half of the marital assets."

He snorted. "Only if she contributed half, which isn't the way things work, and you know it."

"You have a very low opinion of women."

"I love women, but I'm realistic."

Lorna came to a full stop. "Have you ever been in love?"

"Of course. I told you, I almost got married."

"And you loved her?"

He paused, his brow wrinkling as he considered the question. "I wanted to marry her."

"That's not the same thing. How did you feel when the relationship ended?"

"What do you mean?"

"Were you hurt? Upset? Did you feel lost?"

"Listen, if you think I'm an unfeeling jerk—"

"Answer the question. What did you feel after the breakup?"

He didn't respond right away. They stood feet apart and simply looked at each other. She could almost see the wheels turning in his head as he wondered if this conversation was a trap. But she wasn't trying to trap him. She really wanted to get insight into how he viewed relationships and get a better understanding of his feelings.

"I cared about Bria, but by then, the relationship had run its course, and I was focused on building my business. When we broke up, I wasn't torn up, I felt..." He hesitated to finish the sentence.

"Relieved?" Lorna supplied.

"Yes," he bit out. "I'm not proud of it, but if you're looking for someone to lie to you, that's not me. I'm honest and upfront. That's important, don't you think?"

Lorna gazed at him for a second. "Very important," she said, and started walking again.

6

They tossed their empty cups in a trash bin.

"What do you want to do now?" Reginald asked.

Lorna smiled but could feel the fakeness and was certain Reginald noticed because she had a hard time hiding her true feelings on her face. Her sister often called her face *expressive*, using a sarcastic tone when she did.

She took a deep breath and released it, wondering how to get out of this awkward situation. The night had started well, and she'd anticipated sleeping with him, but their conversation had killed the inclination. They'd talked about other things, of course.

She told him about her love for collecting music boxes, and he told her he used to be a long-distance runner for his high school track team. He let the sport go when he attended college but took up running again in recent years. Now he ran 10k races for fun and was training for one coming up in April. He was a lover of the arts and liked attending local art shows. That tidbit excited her for a split second because she loved art too and regularly attended shows.

Yet none of those interesting facts shook off her unease

about Reginald. She was a romantic at heart, and he was clearly a cynic. Sometimes finding your opposite could be a good experience. You learned from each other and different ideas could enrich a relationship. She didn't see that happening in this case.

"I'm going home," Lorna said.

Reginald's eyebrows shot up in surprise. "Right now? It's not that late. We could—"

"No, I'm going home. I have things to do in the morning." She made a big show of pulling her keys out of her shoulder bag.

Reginald frowned. "Okay. I'll walk you to your car."

Lorna's smile was swift and tight. "Not necessary. I parked in the deck, and it's well lit."

"There's no way I'm letting a woman walk back to her car by herself. My momma raised me better than that."

"You're not responsible for me, Reggie. It's not necessary. Really. I promise not to tell your momma. I'll be fine." Lorna showed him the mace on her key chain.

The frown on his brow deepened. "If I didn't know better, I'd think you were trying to get rid of me."

He was straightforward, so she would be too. "If that's what you think, then you'd be right."

"Excuse me?"

She breathed a heavy sigh, gearing up to tell him what she really thought. "You like honesty, so I'm going to give it to you straight. I appreciate what you did for me, and I hope dinner was enough compensation, but I really don't want to see you again. You're not exactly what I expected."

He stiffened. "What did you expect?"

His question prompted her to evaluate her own thought processes. What had she expected? Clearly, she'd projected her own wants and desires onto him. The truth was, she was looking for Mr. Right, and she'd created a scenario in her head where their reconnection meant they were supposed to be together.

Embarrassing, to say the least. He'd literally saved her, and with a last name like Knight, how was she not supposed to think that somehow fate had intervened and blessed her with another opportunity to fall in love?

But she had been wrong.

"I expected you to be kind and—"

"I am kind," Reginald interrupted, sounding offended.

"You are, to a point," Lorna said slowly, choosing her words carefully. "But you make disparaging remarks about women and love."

He ran a hand over the crown of his head. "Let's start over. Maybe you misunderstood what I meant."

"I heard you loud and clear, and I didn't misunderstand. I'm sure you'll make the perfect partner. For someone else."

He let out a short laugh and folded his arms across his chest. "What were you looking for? Oh, let me guess, you thought you had found a man you could sucker into a relationship with words about love and forever, am I right?"

She let out a high-pitched laugh, which caused him to stare at her as if she'd grown an eye in the middle of her forehead. "Sucker? Everyone on the planet is looking for love. I happened to be looking in the wrong place. You think you're quite the catch, and a woman like me should be glad you're interested. Did I get that right?"

"I never said anything like that, but if the shoe fits." Reginald shrugged.

Lorna slammed her fist onto her hips. "You're a chauvinistic pig, and don't you worry about anyone wanting half of your crap. I seriously doubt you can find a woman who would even want to marry you. At any rate, I pray no one is foolish enough to do that because they'll be miserable until they can escape your clutches."

"You're the one who wanted to be in my clutches," he said between clenched teeth.

"You wish."

"I know an interested woman when I see one, and you planned to seduce me tonight."

Lorna let out a loud laugh and plastered her hand against her chest as if she had heard the funniest joke in history. Stepping closer to him she lowered her voice. "Only a desperate woman would sleep with you," she said sweetly.

"I knew you were desperate." He didn't flinch.

Lorna itched to slap him but refrained. She would not resort to violence. Instead, she straightened her spine and stared him right in the eyes.

"I'm not desperate, but I was definitely willing. Now that I've gotten to know you, you killed any chance of us hooking up. Great job, genius."

His face fell, and she smirked when he realized he had been the one to destroy the opportunity for them to get horizontal.

"I'll take my desperate behind home to my nice warm bed. I'm not wasting my time or my body on a man like you."

Lorna traced a hand down the middle of his chest, encountering hard muscle which made her catch her breath and almost change her mind. Instead, she doubled down on her smirk and nonchalant attitude, refusing to give him the satisfaction of knowing that she too regretted that they couldn't get horizontal tonight. She'd actually been looking forward to it after a dry spell.

"Have a good night." She swung on her heel and marched off, definitely conflicted. While she felt good about giving him a piece of her mind, her lady parts throbbed with awareness.

The man was fine in the face and touching his chest confirmed he had a great body to match. Why did he have to open his mouth and spoil the night?

With brisk strides, she entered the public parking deck and

went to her car. She pulled into traffic with more aggression than necessary. From the corner of her eye, she thought she saw Reginald, but that didn't make sense. He'd walked away from her and gone in the opposite direction.

Her mind was playing tricks.

She pushed on the accelerator, unable to get away from there fast enough.

AT HOME and changed into comfortable pajamas, Lorna poured herself a glass of wine and sat on the sofa with one leg curled under her. She called Glory, her older sister in Pennsylvania.

Her sister answered on the second ring.

"Hey, why are you calling me? Aren't you supposed to be on a hot date with the guy you knew back in college?"

She sounded upbeat and optimistic, and Lorna was almost sorry to disappoint her.

"I told you it wasn't a date, and I'm glad I didn't get my hopes up. Well, not too much anyway."

"That doesn't sound good. How did things go?" Glory asked.

"Not as I'd hoped. We had a nice dinner and then went to have ice cream. Over the course of the evening, it became clear to me that Reggie is a lot more cynical now than back in college. I never imagined he had such a low opinion of women."

She heard the rustle of bedsheets as her sister moved around. "Uh-oh, what did he do?"

Lorna gave her sister the highlights of the night, and Glory listened without interrupting. She understood Lorna needed to vent. Being only a couple of years apart, they were very close and knew each other well.

"I'm sorry that happened to you," Gloria said. "I know you

were really looking forward to tonight. I had my hopes up for you as well."

"Well, those have been dashed, and it's just as well. I don't want to spend time with someone who thinks women are the devil. I'm paraphrasing."

"Yikes."

"By the way, I don't think there's anything wrong with doing divorce parties, but he's way too cynical. I would've loved to get to know him better, but he's not right for me. I'm not sure he's right for anyone."

"I know you're disappointed by how the night turned out, but it's probably for the best. Better you know now than get your heart broken later."

"True. I'm not giving up, though. Reggie wasn't the one for me, but I believe there is someone else out there. The best thing I can do is not waste my time with men like him who aren't looking for or interested in love."

"Amen. Stay focused on what you want, and you should be able to find happiness again."

"Thanks for listening to me vent. I hope I didn't interrupt your night."

"You interrupted my night, but he'll be all right."

Lorna shook her head and laughed. Unlike her, her sister was not looking for Mr. Right. She was enjoying Mr. Right Now —her latest paramour in a string of lovers she'd become involved with ever since a messy divorce ended her marriage several years ago. Because of that, she was not interested in getting married again.

"I'll let you go now."

"I'll keep my fingers crossed for you."

"Thanks, sis. Bye."

After they hung up, Lorna swirled the wine in her glass. Too bad Reginald turned out to not be what she was looking for. She wished she could be like her sister and not care about his personality—use him for sex until she found her Mr. Right. But she wasn't like Glory at all.

Reginald was a no go because she'd learned a tough lesson years ago. She was not going to waste her time. Not even on someone as appealing as him.

7

The basketball bounced off Reginald's chest and was quickly retrieved by Axel Beck of the opposing team. Dark-skinned and bearded, the tall attorney dribbled toward the net and leaped in the air for a smooth slam dunk.

He landed on his feet and thumped his chest. "Booyah! Game!" He and his teammates high-fived each other.

"What the hell, Reggie?" Chase yelled, arms spread wide, mouth open in disgust.

Axel, Colton, and Braxton were friends they'd met at Double Trouble. They were great basketball players, having won trophies at leagues they played in around the city. For the longest time, Reginald and his cousins had wanted to play against them. Today was that day, and it was a massacre.

They whooped Reginald, Chase, and Xavier with a score of twenty to ten, which was Reginald's fault. He couldn't concentrate, which was Lorna's fault.

"Shoulda quit while you were ahead." Axel tossed the ball to Xavier.

"Next time," Chase grumbled.

Their three opponents chuckled.

Axel pointed at them. "Don't forget you owe us drinks and dinner at Double Trouble Friday night."

"Don't you have a fiancée to spend time with?" Reginald demanded, annoyed.

"Don't worry about my woman. Naphressa will understand I need to claim my free meal. Make sure you have enough money to cover the tab. I drink a lot and have a hearty appetite." Backing away, Axel smirked and patted his stomach before leaving the gym with his friends.

Reginald felt eyes on him. When he turned his head, both Chase and Xavier were glowering at him.

"Care to tell us what's going on?" Chase asked, crossing his arms over his chest.

"Please provide plenty of detail for why you got our asses handed to us in a game of basketball."

Xavier sounded disgusted, and understandably so. He coached teen basketball and had played ball himself back in high school. Reginald's poor performance and their subsequent loss cut deep.

"I can't concentrate." Reginald trudged toward the bleachers.

He hadn't stopped thinking about Lorna. When she walked away from him, he went in the opposite direction and then felt guilty, swung around, and followed her to the parking deck. Keeping his distance, he watched until she safely pulled out of the lot before going to his own car. He was angry, but he wasn't a dick.

On the drive home, he went over everything that had happened in his mind and realized he had been too honest. He had gotten too comfortable, but hell, that wasn't his fault. Lorna was easy to talk to.

"Why can't you concentrate?" Xavier asked.

Reginald climbed to the middle of the bleachers and sat down. "You'll never believe me if I tell you."

Xavier walked over, wiping sweat off his brow. "Try me."

"Don't laugh, but remember I told you I was going out with Lorna Saturday night?"

"Yeah, what happened?" Chase sat two rows below Reginald and chugged water.

"I messed up."

He launched into a recounting of the night—the delicious meal, the great conversation, and then the way everything fell apart during their walk around the courthouse square. He included how he berated himself on the ride home.

Despite telling his cousins not to laugh, they both had a good chuckle at his expense.

"You have got to be kidding me. The Green-Eyed Bandit messed up?" Chase asked.

"Must be the end of days," Xavier deadpanned.

"Are you both done now?" Reginald asked.

"Wait, I have one more," Xavier said. "When you step to a woman, make sure you step right."

That was cold. He had used one of Reginald's own sayings against him. He hadn't used that statement in a long time but had definitely said it in the past.

His cousins fell out laughing, high-fiving each other before they finally quieted down.

"Okay, okay, we're done now. How are you going to fix your screw up?" Chase asked. "You can't continue like this. You had a crappy game and now we owe those guys dinner and drinks. Call Lorna, apologize, and try again. You obviously like her a lot."

Reginald snorted. He might feel terrible, but he hadn't done anything wrong. "Apologize for what? For being my true authentic self? That's what women say they want."

"They want your true authentic self, but you yourself

admitted that you might have come on a little too strong right away. Invite her to dinner to make up for your behavior."

"Then she'll think I'm trying to get in her pants."

"Aren't you?" Xavier quirked an eyebrow.

"Yes and no. The truth is, I kind of enjoyed spending time with her."

There was a moment of silence.

"Whoa. I don't know the last time I've heard you say that about a woman," Xavier said.

"I don't know the last time I said it. There's something about her, and I can't put my finger on what makes her keep my attention in a way no other woman has. Maybe it's because she's so... friendly. She's practically the same woman I met back in college. That friendliness can't be faked, right? We know women are the greatest actresses in the world."

"*You* do. I'm not as jaded as you are," Chase said.

"Me either," Xavier added.

"Nonetheless, you know the business I run. I see women running circles around men all day, every day. I see these brokenhearted bastards trying to pick up the pieces of their shattered lives after their wives leave them, each one believing his wife was the real deal."

"Maybe Lorna's the real deal. You'll never know unless you give it a try," Xavier said.

"Too late for that now."

Trying sounded much easier than it was. He believed to really know someone, you needed to date for a long period of time. Even after that, there was no guarantee you and the other person were compatible, but the chance of success increased.

Xavier was right. Unless he tried, he wouldn't know if Lorna was the right kind of woman for him, but part of him was afraid to reach for the type of relationship he wanted. Bria's demands lingered in the recesses of his mind, and he knew, better than his cousins, how devastating breakups could be.

He'd been a counselor, therapist, and confidant to hundreds of men over the years. Despite the front they put on to friends, those guys were hurting. Some of them had literally cried at their divorce party. He didn't want to be that guy—crying at a party because he was finally feeling some type of happiness again after the crushing blow of losing the woman he loved.

But, could he risk *not* taking the chance? What if Lorna was different? What if *they* could be different? Maybe, like his cousin suggested, he should try.

"You guys want to grab some lunch?" Chase asked, rising to his feet.

"I could eat," Xavier said.

They both turned their attention to Reginald.

He stood. "You guys go ahead. I'm going to head home, and I have a few errands to run. I'll catch up with you later."

"All right, man."

He watched his cousins walk out of the gym. Once they left, he took a deep breath and dialed Lorna's number. He didn't quite know what he was going to say, but he wanted to at least reach out and let her know that he had screwed up and, if she was interested, he wanted to start again.

Except, when he dialed her number, there was a single ring and then it went to voicemail. He walked out to the car. Sitting in the driver seat, he sent a text.

By the time he arrived at home, there was no acknowledgement of either the voicemail or the text. As he strolled into the house, he kept his eyes pinned to the phone screen. Nothing. No confirmation that the call had been delivered. Now that was odd.

Then it dawned on him what was wrong. She had blocked his number.

Damn.

8

A blocked number was no match for his determination. Reginald returned to the coffee shop Lorna had entered the day they ran into each other. He went back every day around the same time he had seen her that morning. Every day, he ordered an espresso with an extra shot and sat in the corner for at least thirty minutes, hoping to run into her.

As two days turned into three, and six days turned to seven, he began to lose hope. Maybe he should give up. There were plenty of women out there who would be happy to go out with him.

Hell, who was he kidding? He wanted her. She remained on his mind as certainly as if she had pulled up a chair and sat down.

Lorna had captured his attention, wormed her way under his skin, and made him regret the words he said, and the fact that she had blocked his number bothered him more than he cared to admit.

On day fifteen, a Friday, more than two weeks after he had begun frequenting the shop, he entered and told himself this would be the last time. Driving to Marietta every day during the week had been an exercise in futility. A waste of time and gas.

He had to get up early every morning to make the long trek, hang around long enough to make sure she didn't come in, and then drive his lame ass to work. If a male friend had told him what he was doing, he'd call him pathetic—and that's exactly how he felt. Pathetic. Even worse, twice he thought he saw her, but he'd made a mistake.

Reginald entered the shop, and the door closed behind him. As he scanned the small space, he pulled up short. Lo and behold, standing in line was a woman with a short haircut and wearing a yellow peacoat.

His heart leapt into his throat, and he could hardly breathe. What the heck was wrong with him? He hooked a finger in the top of his shirt and tugged on the collar. He was acting like a crazy fan meeting their idol, but that's exactly how he felt. His heart was racing, his hands were sweaty, and blood buzzed in his ears.

The door behind him opened and closed, and a man in a suit strode by. Jolted into action, Reginald rushed ahead of him.

"Excuse me," he said, edging in front.

The customer frowned but fortunately didn't make a big deal out of Reginald's actions.

Rolling his neck, he summoned a basic greeting that wouldn't let Lorna know how excited he was to see her.

"Lorna, is that you?"

She glanced over her shoulder, and their eyes met. The same heat from the night of their dinner came over him. He had it bad. He was practically jonesing for her.

"Hi." A dry, unenthusiastic greeting. No emotion in her voice.

She faced the front again, as if they didn't know each other. As if they hadn't sat down to dinner and had a great conversation, enjoyed ice cream as they strolled through Decatur, and then argued before going their separate ways. Granted, the night had not ended the way he wanted, and it did not go the way she had wanted, but they weren't strangers for goodness' sake.

"I haven't been here in a minute. I can't believe we ran into each other. How have you been?" he asked.

Her shoulders lifted and fell as she took a deep breath. She turned her head sideways, refusing to face him directly and only giving a view of her profile.

"Fine," she answered in a clipped tone.

This was not going well.

He figured she might still be upset, but she seemed more than upset, which made him realize he had more work to do than expected.

"I've been fine too, thanks for asking."

She shot another look over her shoulder. "I don't know what you want me to say. We didn't exactly part on good terms."

Reginald rocked forward so his lips came close to her ear. "We could simply talk, like normal people do." She smelled delicious, like sweet honey and... did he detect cinnamon? He wanted to take a bite of her to find out if she tasted as sweet and spicy as she smelled.

Her gaze dipped lower. "What do you want to talk about?"

Progress! Yeah, baby.

"How have you been?"

"I already answered that question."

They shuffled forward in the line.

"How have you *really* been? What have you been up to the past couple of weeks? How is business? Ate at any good restaurants you might want to recommend?"

Her gaze slid sideways, climbing from the middle of his torso to his face. He felt that look deep in his chest and low in his pelvis.

"I really have been fine. Busy at work. Things are picking up because spring is around the corner, which is when a lot of people renew their vows. I haven't eaten at any new restaurants recently, but if you know of any you can recommend, I'd love to hear about it."

The line moved again, and he almost pumped his fist. He was definitely making progress. If he was reading her right, that comment at the end was a little flirty.

"I might know about a place, assuming you like Thai food."

"I am a fan of Thai," she said.

"Well in that case—"

The customer in front of her finished paying, and Lorna walked up to the counter and placed her order. When she finished, Reginald stepped up to the counter while she moved to the left.

Before he could give his order, the male barista asked, "The usual?"

The question took him by surprise. Considering he had pretended to Lorna that he hadn't been back since they met, and their meeting should be seen as a coincidence, he almost reached across the counter and shook the young man.

"I don't know what you're talking about."

The young man frowned. "You come in here every day."

Lorna shot Reginald a look, raising an eyebrow.

Reginald laughed off the comment. "You have me confused with someone else. I'll have a plain coffee, black."

Normally he ordered an espresso, but he couldn't do that since the barista had called him out. Moron.

"Whatever," the young man mumbled, ringing up the order.

Reginald paid for his coffee and then stepped aside to stand next to Lorna. A woman behind the counter called her name, and she picked up her drink and went to the stand where the napkins and other items were located.

Reginald kept his eyes on her while he waited for his coffee.

If necessary, he'd abandon his drink to catch her before she left.

Right as she headed toward the door, his order came up. He snatched the cup and hurried toward the exit. Outside, he called her name before she could rush off.

"Lorna."

She paused, looking at him with curiosity in her eyes.

"I know I screwed up the night we went out, but I meant what I said about the Thai restaurant, if you're interested. I'm hoping you'll give me another shot to make a first impression."

She didn't respond right away, studying him with slightly narrowed eyes. "Why should I bother?" she finally asked.

"Because you have the wrong idea about me after that night, and I want to change your opinion. I'm actually a pretty good guy."

"Just cynical." Not a question, but a statement.

"Cautious," he suggested.

Her lips quirked into a soft smile. "Why do I feel like I'm going to regret this?"

"You're not. If I'm not mistaken, you were interested in me until I put my foot in my mouth. Am I wrong?"

She pursed her lips. "You're not wrong, but right now I'm not so sure."

"Give me another shot. If after we go out again you still feel the same way, I'll leave you alone."

"Why do you want to go out with me again?"

Good question. He wasn't sure what the answer was. All he knew was that he liked this woman—*a lot.* He'd denied to his cousins how much, but back in college, he'd been enamored. If she'd given him a shot, he would have set aside every other woman to be with her—and that wasn't easy to admit.

He didn't want her last memory of him to be of the two of them having an argument. *If* that was going to be the last memory. But *if* he got his way, it wouldn't be.

"You're not just trying to get in my panties, are you?"

"I'm absolutely trying to get into your panties."

One of her eyebrows lifted higher.

"Would you rather I lie?" he asked.

"No, I guess not. You really are upfront and honest, aren't you?"

"It's better that way." He stepped closer. "I'm pretty sure you want me in your panties, but that's not the primary reason for me asking you out. I enjoyed our conversation, and now that I know to stay away from the topics of marriage and relationships, maybe we can have a good time."

"We don't have to stay away from those topics," she said.

"I think we do."

"No, we don't. You said some troubling things, but that's your opinion based on experience." She shrugged. "The same way my opinion is different from yours, based on my experience. I'm not saying we have to talk about marriage or relationships again, but if the topic comes up, I'll try not to be so sensitive. And who knows, maybe I can change your mind."

He laughed softly. "Since I want you to accept my invitation, no comment. You're open to going to the Thai restaurant?"

After a moment's hesitation, she nodded. "Yes. When?"

"Why wait? I'm free tomorrow night. Are you?"

"A friend of mine is displaying his work at a gallery tomorrow, and I'm going to support him. You like art. Would you like to meet me there?"

"I'd love to. Then we'll go to dinner after?"

"Sounds good to me."

"So you'll take my calls now, right?"

She laughed. "Yes, Reggie, I'll take your calls now."

"Let me see you unblock my number."

"Are you serious?"

"Let me see."

"Fine." She took out her phone and showed him on the screen that she'd unblocked his number. "There."

"Thank you. Now text me the information for the gallery."

"You're so bossy," she mumbled, but she did as he asked.

The information popped up on his screen. "Perfect. I'll see you tomorrow night."

"Okay," she said, this time blessing him with the prettiest, cutest smile. It didn't only rest on her lips. The smile took over her cheeks and made her brown eyes turn bright and friendly.

They walked away from each other, but he kept an eye on her from the corner of his eye. He saw when she went into her vehicle, and by the time he climbed behind the wheel of his silver Jaguar, he had already sent a text to his cousins to let them know about the development.

Then he pulled out of the parking lot in a much better mood than he had been in for weeks.

9

The prestigious Noble Art Gallery had three locations in the city. The showing was at the Midtown location, and when Lorna arrived the place was already packed.

Her friend, Eric McBride, had worked hard for years to have his photography taken seriously. He started out as an assistant to a more famous photographer before striking out on his own and opening his own studio, where he did weddings and other noteworthy events. This was only his second exhibition, and he was nervous.

She arrived earlier than she told Reginald because she wanted to see Eric first and share encouraging words. She dressed simply in a forest green sweater dress with three-quarter length sleeves and a high neckline. It molded to her curves. It was casual but became dressy with the colorful scarf and bulky jewelry she wore.

The other artists with work on display included two painters and a ceramic artist. She admired their work as she strolled through the venue, keeping an eye out for Eric. She found him explaining his work to an audience of four. When he saw her, he paused, a faint smile coming to his lips before he informed them how he'd come to take that specific photograph —storm clouds—over the tops of buildings.

When he finished, he immediately came to her, and she gave him a hug.

"I'm so glad you could make it," he said, looking at her through black glasses.

They'd known each other for years and dated for a short period before he asked her to marry him two years ago. She turned him down, but they remained friends—supporting each other through the various trials and tribulations of life. Seeing him succeed after working so hard for so long made her very happy.

"Where else would I be? Your work is amazing. I think you get better every time I see new shots."

"Oh, come on."

"No, I'm serious." Lorna hugged his arm and pointed. "Like the one you were talking about a second ago. I haven't seen that before, but you captured the pending chaos of the clouds and their natural beauty against the stark, man-made buildings."

He nodded, gazing at the work as if seeing it for the first time. "The different textures, the light... You see that?"

"Absolutely."

His eyes looked warmly at her. "That's the great thing about you. You always see my vision, and you always understand my work. You don't know how much I appreciate that."

"I do, because it's not the first time that you've told me so."

"So, where is this man of yours?" He tossed a gaze around the room.

"I want you to be nice."

"I'm always nice."

She laughed. "No, you're not, but I'm going to let that slide. He should be here shortly. I wanted to spend some time checking out the work and making sure you're okay."

"Look at you, always worried about other folks." He placed an arm around her shoulder and squeezed her into his side. "I'm good. Definitely calmer than when I first arrived, but it's good to see you. Your smile helped push me the last of the distance."

"That's what I'm here for. Support."

He took her hand. "Come on, there's one photograph I want to show you. I know you're going to love it."

The piece he showed her was as striking as he said. A black and white close up of an older Black woman, age forming lines in her face like the tributaries of a river. He managed to capture the wisdom in her eyes and the wariness of life in her face.

Eric was truly a gifted artist. Though their relationship hadn't worked out, Lorna was as proud as any girlfriend would be of his work and accomplishments.

Sometime later, she idled near the refreshment table eating a piece of cheese on a toothpick, when Reginald strolled into the gallery. Struck by his appearance, she caught her breath.

Several heads turned in his direction. He was impressive in a black shirt and tan slacks. A knot of tension entered her stomach, and she watched him for a moment. His gaze slid through the room, searching for her, but she eased behind a group of people so he couldn't see her while she observed him.

Why had she agreed to go out with him again?

Yes, he was charming. Yes, he was downright fine. His attractiveness sank its fingers into her and forced her to pay attention to his every movement.

But they were not in sync with what they wanted out of a relationship, so she should run in the opposite direction. Except that was the last thing she wanted to do—run from Reginald. She wanted to run *to* him, and if her tightening nipples were any indication, she wanted to do much more than run. She wanted to climb on top of him and see if he lived up to her fantasy.

She hadn't forgotten the press of her hips into his when she lay on top of him in the street. The warm heat from his loins and the firmness of his thighs remained ingrained in her memory. She ached to see him naked and experience the fullness of his possession.

Whew. This man definitely had her mind going crazy.

Reginald headed off to the right, and she followed.

"Reggie!"

He turned, and the minute he saw her, his face broke into a smile, turning her insides into quivering gelatin.

"Hey, there," he said in a slow drawl, gaze skimming her outfit with blatant appreciation. That was exactly the reaction she'd wanted, and her skin prickled under the heat of his gaze.

He pulled her into a one-armed hug, and the brief brush of their bodies against each other sparked a flame inside of her. Not out of control yet, but definitely with the potential to become unmanageable.

"Which of the works is your friend's?" he asked, keeping a light hand at her back.

"The photographs. He's extremely talented."

"I see. He does a good job not only capturing landscapes, but capturing emotion in the faces of his subjects."

She nodded, pleased he noticed. "Let me see if I can find him and introduce you."

They found Eric talking to a young couple and waited until he wrapped up the conversation.

He approached, extending a hand and a friendly smile. "So you're Reggie."

Both men shook hands.

"That's me. I was enjoying your work. Quite impressive."

"If you see anything you like, I'll give you the friend and family discount because of Lorna."

"You don't have to do that, but I'm not going to turn down a deal."

They all three laughed.

"Listen, I've got to continue mingling, but it was nice to meet you. Take good care of my girl, will you?"

"Would you stop," Lorna said, gently slapping Eric's arm.

"What is it people say? I want you to be happy, even if it's not with me."

He gave her a kiss on the cheek and then walked away.

Reginald's gaze swung to her. "What did he mean by that?"

"What?"

"Were you and he together at some point?"

"A couple of years ago, but we're only friends now. Ready to see the rest of his work?"

He watched her closely, and she thought he was about to question her more, but instead said, "Sure, lead the way."

They spent another thirty minutes walking through the gallery. Reginald didn't purchase any of the photographs, but he did end up purchasing a painting.

After the gallery assistant wrapped the piece, he asked if she was ready to eat.

"Definitely. I tried not to spoil my appetite with these hors d'oeuvres, so I'm ready."

"I am too. I need to put this in the car, and then I'll be ready to go."

She followed him to his vehicle, and he placed the painting in the trunk.

"When you gave me the address, I changed my mind about the Thai restaurant. There are quite a few restaurants nearby, and I found a place called Soul Kitchen. If you're really in the mood for Thai, we can go somewhere else, but this place is within walking distance."

"I'll let you lead the way," Lorna said.

They strolled down the sidewalk, chatting about the artwork they saw. When they arrived, the restaurant was mostly empty.

"Are you sure the food is good?" she asked.

He laughed. "The online reviews are mostly positive, but they haven't been open very long so there aren't a lot of people who know about the location. We're sort of pioneers. If it's as good as the comments online, once word gets out, getting in here like this on a Friday night is going to become a thing of the past."

Lorna groaned. "Don't you hate when a spot you love becomes popular? Great for the business but bad for us pioneers, as you put it. Guess we better enjoy it while we can."

They entered and ordered their meals and drinks, and then Reginald sat back and simply stared at her.

"What?"

"I'm still surprised you agreed to go out with me again. But I'm glad you did," he quickly added.

"You were very convincing." Lorna spread the white napkin across her thighs.

"Did I have to convince you, or were you a little bit interested in seeing me again?"

"Somebody is fishing for compliments."

He threw up his hands. "Guilty as charged."

His answer surprised her. She expected him to pretend otherwise, but that wasn't the case. She shouldn't be surprised. Reginald was very direct, and she appreciated his honesty.

"Well then, the least I can do is be honest and let you know that, yes, I was interested in seeing you again."

His lips spread into a knowing smile.

"Get that look off your face."

"I can't help but be happy, so that's going to be hard to do." He rested his forearms on the table. "What's the deal with you and Eric? You two still have a thing going?"

"No, I told you, he's in the past."

"How serious did you get?" he asked.

Lorna let out a deep breath. "He asked me to marry him."

Reginald's eyebrows shot toward the ceiling.

"Don't give me that look," she chided him.

"Is there a possibility that you might still be interested in him?"

She kept eye contact. "Absolutely not."

"And you were together only a couple of years ago?"

"Don't you believe a man and woman can be friends?"

"Maybe, but I don't make a habit of keeping female friends. Especially ones I've slept with. It's obvious he's still interested in you."

"He's not interested in me."

"You're sure about that?"

"I'm certain."

"What about that remark he made about wanting you to be happy, even if it's not with him?"

"He meant it, but I've known him a long time, and we're well past any awkward stage. We're really good friends who support each other. He's a great guy. Very talented. McBride Photography Studio, his business, does excellent work, as you saw."

"He's talented. He's a great guy. If he's so great, why didn't you marry him?"

She paused. "I loved him, but not in that way, and to be honest, when I thought I'd lose his friendship, it terrified me. Terrified me so much I almost changed my mind and said yes. But I knew we weren't meant to be together as a couple. I feel as if... when you know, you know, and I knew we weren't supposed to be together. Once he got over his feelings being hurt, Eric agreed that I was right. We've been good friends ever since."

"If you say so," Reginald said.

But by the way he spoke, she knew he didn't mean it.

10

After a delicious meal, they slowly strolled to their vehicles in the parking lot. Only a few people remained inside the gallery. Reginald didn't see Eric, but he figured he was probably somewhere out of sight.

The conversation went a lot better this time. Reginald didn't want the night to end, and as he walked Lorna to her car, he suspected she felt the same way. At least he hoped she did.

They stopped at her car. "I had a really good time. What did you think of your meal?" Lorna asked.

"I enjoyed it, and the conversation was better," Reginald said, stuffing his hands into his pants pockets.

"A lot better," Lorna agreed, her eyes narrowing in amusement.

"Where are you going now?"

"Home. And you?"

She gazed up at him under the lights in the parking lot. He had a sudden urge to kiss her but refrained from the tug of her lips.

"I want to get into something else. Are you up to go dancing?"

Her eyes widened. "I don't know the last time I went dancing."

"Yeah, me either." He paused, looking her directly in the eyes. "Let me be real with you. I don't want to let you go yet. What do you think about that?"

Reginald wasn't one to beat around the bush, and he didn't want to walk away from the chemistry between them yet.

"I like the idea of spending a little more time together, and I'm definitely open to going dancing. Where did you have in mind?"

"How about Club Masquerade? I haven't been there in a while, but I have a great time whenever I go."

Club Masquerade was the hottest club in Atlanta and bound to be busy even at this early hour because they not only offered hot music and a popular VIP section, the club served gourmet Southern cuisine with a modern twist.

"I've been there. It's a nice place, and they have great food—not that I want to eat again," Lorna hastily added.

"At least if we get hungry, we know the food will be delicious, which is unusual for club food."

"So true."

"So you're up for it?"

"Yes, I'm up for it."

"Excellent. Follow me."

They drove out of the parking lot, and Reginald led the way to the club. When they arrived, he escorted Lorna to the front entrance, and they entered the multi-story building. Inside, gyrating bodies moved around the dance floor. An escalator took guests to an upper floor, and blue, purple, and red strobe lights flashed across the ceiling while the latest hip-hop beat bumped through the speakers.

They found seats at the bar and Reginald ordered a Jack Daniels and Coke and a white wine for Lorna.

"Don't tell me I'm so predictable you already know what I'll drink."

"Okay, I won't tell you how predictable you are." He rested one hand on the back of her stool and faced her. The alluring scent of her skin and perfume filled his nostrils, and he longed to nuzzle her neck. He resisted the urge and instead simply gazed at her pretty profile.

Lorna crossed legs toward him. "Why do you think you haven't been to a club in a while?"

"I don't know. I enjoy myself when I do come."

"Same, and I was trying to figure out why I haven't been in a long time. I realized it's because my circle is shrinking."

"What do you mean?"

"My friend circle. I have the same friends, but they all have different priorities now. We're all in our mid-thirties, and the women I used to go out with are married and/or have children, so they don't have the time or desire to go clubbing."

Reginald considered what she said. "You know what, now that you mention it, except for my cousins, most of the men I know are married and have kids too. That would probably explain why it's been a minute since I've been to the club. But now that I know you like it, I'll make sure I ask you from now on."

"So I'm sort of your club escort?"

"Yeah, something like that."

"Club standby?" she suggested.

"Club partner," he added.

She giggled and took a sip of her wine, eyeing him playfully.

"Uh-oh. What's that expression?" Reginald asked.

Did she have any idea how sexy she looked? Damn near made him want to hand in his player card and hand *her* his credit card. He was dealing with a dangerous woman. The kind that could have a man falling in love and begging for forgiveness for shit he didn't even do—just to stay in her good graces.

"Tell me something about you that would surprise me," Lorna said.

"I can't think of anything. I'm a boring party planner."

"Yeah, right. You seem... I don't know, like even though you're forthright and upfront, it's as if you're holding secrets."

"Really? Huh."

"Yes. I want to get to know you better, Reggie—if you'll let me."

She placed a hand on his thigh, and the light touch jump-started a fire in his veins. Tension twisted at the base of his spine.

"Something that would surprise you, huh?"

"Mhmm." She sipped her wine.

Reginald thought for a moment. "Okay, I've never been in love."

Her mouth fell open. "Never?"

"Not once."

"What about Bria?"

"In Decatur, when you asked me about my feelings for her, I wasn't sure, but after some thought I have to accept that I wasn't in love with her. Marriage just seemed like the next logical step for us."

She poked out her lower lip. "That's sad."

He chuckled uneasily, his chest growing warm under her scrutiny. He'd said too much. He shifted in the chair.

"Don't you want to fall in love?" Lorna asked.

She hadn't stopped looking at him, but he couldn't look at her. He should have picked something else to say, but she had an ease about her that made him want to bare his soul and admit all kinds of secrets.

"Maybe. One day. I don't know. Sometimes it seems like it's

more trouble than it's worth. I think people rush into serious commitments before they get to know a person."

He swallowed the last of his cocktail and placed the empty glass on the bar. He signaled to the bartender for another drink.

"You're afraid of being hurt," Lorna said.

He twisted his head toward her. "Afraid? No."

"I get it. Love does hurt." She looked unblinkingly at him.

He swallowed and hoped to remove the attention from him with his next words. "Sounds like you have experience."

She pursed her lips and then took a deep breath. "I was madly in love once. I was supposed to get married, but..." She shook her head.

"He broke it off."

"He died."

"Shit." He hadn't expected that.

Lorna nodded. "This was a few years before Eric. When I lost Marcus, I was sad for a long time, but eventually I let go of those feelings. They were suffocating me. That's the thing about sadness and anger and all those negative emotions. They don't just stifle your happiness and keep you from living a full life. They kill you emotionally and eventually... physically. Like stress, sadness and anger can eat you alive. I made the decision not to be eaten alive."

Reginald didn't know what to say. He didn't think he was angry and certainly wasn't sad, but her words struck a chord in him. Had he been holding on to negative emotions because of Bria? Did his career simply reinforce his negative thoughts?

The bartender placed another drink in front of him, but he didn't touch it. He hopped off the stool and took Lorna's hand. "Come on, let's dance."

He led her to the dance floor. They maneuvered their way into the middle of the gyrating bodies and joined in. She was a good dancer, her torso moving in a snakelike, provocative manner, and her hips swaying to the beat.

When she turned around so her back faced his front, he placed a hand on her hips. He knew better than to touch her. He was already semi-hard, and if he pressed against her bottom, no doubt he would become fully erect.

But he wanted to. He wanted to badly.

She flung her hands up and dropped low, then bounced back up and shook her ass in his face.

Goddamn.

She was going to get him into trouble on the dance floor. What did those moves look like in the bedroom?

He slipped an arm around her waist and pulled her back against him, and their bodies continued to sway to the music.

"You better behave," he warned.

She angled her head toward him. "Or what?"

"I'll give you what you're begging for."

He pressed his hard erection into the cleft of her butt cheeks. With his arms around her, he felt the sharp breath she took. They danced the rest of the song in the same position, his arm around her waist, palms itching to cup her full breasts but resisting the urge.

He didn't know how long they stayed out there, but eventually thirst drove them back to the bar.

This time Lorna ordered a limoncello.

"To mix things up," she said, eyes teasing.

Reginald settled on a plain Coke and nudged her into a corner so they could talk.

"What are you doing when we leave here?" he asked.

Lorna shrugged one shoulder. "Probably going to bed."

His dick jumped. "Really? Me too. We should go to bed together."

She let out a laugh, and he laughed too.

"What'd I say that was so funny?" Reginald asked.

"That was real smooth."

He sobered, looking directly into her eyes. "You don't have to come to bed with me, but I don't want the night to end. Come by my place for a drink and more conversation. I promise not to piss you off."

"I don't think you'll piss me off. You've done really well all evening. Vast improvement on the first night we went out."

"Yes." He pumped his fist in victory.

She let out another endearing laugh, and shot him a sideways glance. "Just a drink and conversation?"

"Unless you want to take advantage of me," he said, lowering his voice.

"Will you let me, if I want to?"

"At this point, you can have anything you want." He said that with a straight face to make sure she knew he wasn't joking.

"Okay," she said quietly. "I would love to go to your place for a drink and conversation."

"Perfect."

They left the club hand in hand. Reginald walked her to her car and pressed her back against the cold steel, caging her in with both hands on top of the roof.

He lowered his lips to hers.

Finally.

Her arms slipped around his waist, and she pressed her soft body against his. Fingers curling atop the vehicle, Reginald tasted the limoncello on the tip of her tongue. The bite of the lemony drink was no match for the sweetness of her mouth.

He nipped at her lower lip before sucking the tender flesh. She released a soft whimper, and her warm breath fanned his mouth.

"Ready?" Reginald asked huskily.

She nodded.

11

W hen they entered Reginald's home, they walked into an open floor plan.

"Welcome to my home. Three bedrooms and three baths," he announced.

From the front door, Lorna observed clean lines and right angles and a lot of gray and black. Gray wood floors, gray but comfortable-looking sofas across a black table from each other. Gray-and-white floor length curtains were pulled apart and looked onto the backyard and his neighbors' house, visible above the privacy fence.

"This is nice, but... you kinda need some color in here," Lorna remarked, dropping her purse on a side table.

Reginald chuckled. "You sound like my mother. She said the same thing, but when I told her to help me decorate, she was too busy."

"Too busy doing what?"

"She does a lot of volunteer work. She's a retired schoolteacher and offers tutoring services at the local community center. She's also in a walking club and delivers food to the sick and shut in at her church. You name it, my mom does it."

"Sounds like she lives a very full, active life."

"She does, and she deserves to do whatever she wants. She's worked hard all her life and provided for me on her own after my dad died."

"How old were you when he passed?"

"Thirteen. He'd had heart problems from the time he was a kid, and one day his heart gave out."

"I'm sorry."

"Yeah. He was a good man."

Reginald fell silent for a moment. At odd times, he thought about his father and experienced the pain of loss again as he wondered what life would have been like for them if he'd lived. Luckily, his mother had her sisters to have her back and provide support.

"Both your parents alive?" he asked.

"Yes. Like your mother, they're very active." Lorna's eyes scanned the room. "Didn't you say you like art and collected it?"

"I do and I do."

"I don't see any art on your walls." She turned in a circle, as if a painting would suddenly appear.

"That's because you need to enter my private gallery."

"Excuse me?"

Reginald wore a smug expression on his face. "Follow me."

He picked up the painting he'd brought in from Noble Art Gallery, and Lorna followed him through a doorless entrance. He flipped on the light, and her mouth fell open. He really did have a private gallery. The room was about 10 x 12 with dove gray walls, no windows, and the same dark gray wood floors.

The walls, however, were filled with artwork. Colorful and vibrant paintings of a beautiful sunset, a woman in an electric blue dress suspended in the air in the middle of a pirouette, a field filled with red, yellow, and green tulips. There were more than forty paintings of different sizes on the walls, and like in a gallery, a label beside each one stated the title and the artist.

Hands crossed behind her back, Lorna walked over to a gorgeous abstract painting filled with primary colors. She swiveled on one foot and turned to face Reginald.

"Why?"

"Why what?" He placed the painting he purchased tonight against the wall.

"Why do you have a gallery in your house?"

"Jealousy. When I was a kid, I wanted to be an artist, and my mom always encouraged me. Hyped me up."

She knew where this was going. "But you weren't any good, were you?"

"I sucked, badly." He grimaced.

"I'm so sorry," she said with a laugh.

"Yeah, well, that didn't stop my love for art. I figured if I couldn't paint the images, I could collect them. So that's what I started doing. This is where most of the purchases are located, but I have a few in the bedroom and three in my office at work. I buy mostly local artists—any that catch my eye."

"You're going to run out of room soon."

He laughed. "Then I'll have to turn one of the bedrooms into an overflow gallery."

His gaze rested on one of the pieces, and Lorna took that moment to walk over to him. "You've surprised me for the second time tonight."

"This is what I should've told you when you asked me to tell you something surprising."

"No, I'm glad you were honest about never having been in love. I hope one day you meet someone who can change your mind."

He gazed at her with a thoughtful expression. "I might have already met her."

Silence filled the room as they both absorbed what he'd said. Did he mean that? Or was he simply using the right words to seduce her into bed? If he only knew, he didn't have to try very hard.

"Can I have something to drink, as you promised?" she asked.

"Sure. What can I get you?"

Reginald led the way out of the gallery and back into the main room. In one recessed corner was a stack of bottles filled with different types of liquor and a small cabinet door.

"Surprise me," Lorna said, sitting on the sofa. As she suspected, it was quite comfortable.

"Okay." That one word sounded like a warning.

He opened the cabinet door below and revealed a small refrigerator. Removing ice, he dropped three cubes into a glass.

Lorna couldn't see what he was making, but at the moment she didn't really care. She only had eyes for him and his enticing masculine physique. The tan slacks weren't tight, but they showed off his nice butt. He rolled up the sleeves of the black shirt and revealed arms sprinkled with dark hair.

When he approached her, his green eyes locked with her brown ones, and arousal moistened her panties. Did he really only want to talk? Because she wanted to do more than talk. There was no denying her attraction to him.

She crossed her legs, and when the hem of her sweater dress rode up on her thigh, she didn't pull it down. His gaze shifted to her exposed thigh, but he didn't comment. He handed her a copper mug, and she took a sip of the cocktail.

"Hmm." Lorna coughed a little and tapped her chest.

"You okay?"

She giggled. "I'm fine. The drink was a little stronger than expected."

"Well, you did tell me to surprise you." Reginald sank down next to her.

"What is this?" She took another sip. Now that she was prepared, it didn't hit so hard.

"A Moscow mule."

"I've never had one before. What's in it?"

"Ginger beer and vodka."

"And lime?" she asked.

He nodded. "You like it?"

"Mhmm."

He laughed.

"What are you having?" She leaned toward him, peering into his glass. She wished now she had worn a dress with a lower neckline. She had great cleavage.

"Rum punch." He held out his glass.

Instead of taking it, she held his hand and tilted the glass to her lips. After taking a sip, she gasped. "Oh, that's good. I like that better."

She reached for his glass, but he held it out of reach.

"No, this is mine," Reginald said.

"Come on, can we switch?"

"Nope."

Her mouth fell open. "I'm the guest."

"Well..."

"Pretty please." She batted her eyelids at him.

He laughed. "You're used to getting whatever you want, aren't you?"

"Not always." She sat closer and rested one breast against his biceps. The power emanating from him warmed between her thighs. "Please," she said again, her voice huskier this time.

His eyes dipped to her lips. "I'll let you have it—on one condition."

"What?"

"You let me give you a kiss."

Kissing him was no hardship. The teaser in the parking lot had been delightfully good.

"I can do that."

Reginald leaned toward her, and their lips touched in a

moist, tasty connection. Pleasure shimmied all the way to her toes.

He played with her, nipping the corner of her mouth and lower lip and dipping his tongue between her teeth. She became so lost in the teasing kiss that the mug slipped from her hand and the cocktail spilled onto the floor.

She jumped back and swore softly. "I'm so sorry!"

"Not to worry."

"I'll clean it up. Let me—"

He placed a hand on her arm. "Relax. I'll clean it up. You're the guest, remember?"

She felt horrible about the mess she had made. While Reginald went into the kitchen, she picked up the mug and popped the ice cubes inside it. He came back with a damp towel and sopped up the spilled drink.

He looked at her from his crouched position. "There. All gone."

"You're being awfully kind."

"You want another drink?"

"No, I think I've had enough."

He took the container and went back to the kitchen.

When he returned to the sofa, he wore a smile.

"Thank you for being such an understanding host," Lorna said.

"Not a problem. Now, where were we? Right here, I think?" He leaned toward her.

She leaned toward him. "I think so."

He kissed her again, one arm wound around her waist, and Lorna opened her mouth for the intrusion of his tongue. Their lips fused together while their tongues continued to thrust into and explore each other's mouth.

Reginald pulled her across his lap, and she wound her arms around his neck. The kiss deepened, her mouth opening wide for him. Between her legs was hot and sticky. When his hand slid between her thighs, she spread them for him, desperate for him to touch her there and ease the ache.

Reginald rolled her onto her back against the sofa pillows. Shoving the dress higher, he settled between her thighs, and she could feel his hard erection pressing against her sex. The hard push teased her. Just like his hand was teasing her as it remained unmoving as it cupped her hip.

Restlessly, Lorna twisted against him, grinding her core against the stiff rod in his pants. He showered kisses along her jawline and down to her neck. When his hand reached all the way up and cupped her sex, she jolted from the impact and let out a small cry.

He massaged her lower lips through her panties and made her wetter—made her ache for him to touch her without a barrier. She wanted them to be skin to skin.

"You're so damn wet. I can feel it," he rasped.

She arched her back and spread her legs wider. Reginald nipped at her breasts, tweaking the nipple of the right one with his teeth.

"Reggie," she gasped.

He was going to make her come, fully dressed, from massaging her sex and tormenting her breasts through her dress.

She stared up at the white ceiling with hazy eyes. "Reggie." Her voice cracked on his name.

He shifted and pushed her dress higher. Then he was kissing her inner thigh. His warm breath whispered across her skin as he inched higher. She gripped his shoulders and held on for the storm to come—panting hard, so aroused she couldn't think straight. All she cared about was release.

His teeth dragged along her lower lips, and she came. Hard. With a wail that filled the inside of the large room and bounced off the walls. Over and over climactic waves doused her body in sensation.

When Reginald lifted his head Lorna clutched her chest and stared at him in bewilderment. She couldn't catch her breath. How could she have had such an intense orgasm, fully dressed? What would he do to her once they got naked?

Reginald levered onto his elbows. "Can I take you to bed, Lorna?"

"Yes," she whispered, in a thready voice dripping with want. "Please."

12

The gray interior of Reginald's bedroom was softly lit by square recessed lights, with one shining down on a piece of art anchored above the bed.

"Let me help you out of this," he whispered.

He loosened the scarf from around her neck and it fluttered to the floor. Then he reached around her back and unzipped the sweater dress, which fell to a puddle at her feet.

"Wow," he murmured, eyes roaming her figure.

His reaction was deeply satisfying. She hadn't known how far they'd get tonight but came prepared in a red lace bra that lifted her breasts high, and a matching pair of lace panties.

Lorna slipped off her shoes and reached for the top button on Reginald's shirt. "I should help you out of your clothes too."

"Please do." He smiled as he gazed into her eyes.

She released all the buttons and pushed the shirt off his shoulders. Then he helped her by pulling his undershirt over his head to reveal a firm, tawny chest sprinkled with hair that started at his pecs and disappeared below the waistband of his pants.

"You gonna get the rest of it?" he asked, eyes locked on her face.

"Absolutely." Lorna loosened his belt and unzipped his pants, smiling softly when she noted how his breathing had shortened.

By the time his pants crumbled at his feet, he was sporting an almost fully erect boner in his boxers. They quickly removed their underwear, and she stared at him in awe.

His body was a work of art as magnificent as the pieces hanging on the walls. Firm abs, a muscular chest, and prominent leg muscles that confirmed his penchant for running. And he was, indeed, blessed and highly favored.

With slow, lazy kisses, they made their way to the bed, where Lorna lay back against the pillows and Reginald lowered his bulk between her thighs.

"You're a great kisser," she whispered against his lips.

"So I've been told," he said with a bit of humor and arrogance combined. "You're not too bad yourself."

He kissed his way down her arched throat to the middle of her breasts. Squeezing them together, he sucked the tip of one and then the other, taking his time as if he had all night. He dallied on the left nipple, torturing it until she gasped from unbelievable pleasure.

They rolled onto their sides and faced each other. With gentle, unhurried movements, Reginald caressed her bare back, his hand exploring her butt, hips, and thighs. When his hand returned to her breasts, she drew in a sharp breath. He squeezed the soft flesh and then bent his head to quickly lick the peak before he indulged in another languorous suck.

Lorna fell onto her back and arched into his mouth. Fire coursed through her veins as she lost herself in the pleasure of his touch. Barely able to focus, her head buzzed with dizzying delight while her skin and nerves clamored for more.

Reginald lifted his head, and his green eyes sparkled with

wicked intent. He knew his own power and knew how good he was making her feel. His hands stroked along the curves of her waist and hips, and she writhed on the sheets, lifting her hips in a silent plea to end her torment. His hard flesh nestled against the dark curls between her thighs. Hips slowly circling, he teased her with the promise of possession.

His hands slipped between her legs, and his fingers played with her glistening folds. When he penetrated her core with two fingers, she let out a surprised gasp. Her whole body tensed, and she released a hoarse little moan, gripping his muscular arm and widening her legs.

"Reggie," she breathed, her voice a pained whisper in the darkness of the room.

"I want you to feel so good that you never forget this night, and you never block my number again."

"I promise that I will never—*oh*." Another gasp as he used firmer strokes and added his devilish thumb against her hard and wet clit. She practically vaulted off the bed.

Reginald nipped at her arched throat and then gave the spot a soothing lick. "You promise?"

A trembling breath stuttered past her lips. "Promise."

Lorna clutched his hand and forced his fingers deeper, and Reginald continued to kiss her neck, upper chest, and breasts.

"You're so responsive. You're going to kill me." He sucked on her earlobe.

"I feel like you're killing *me*. Please let me come."

He worked his hands between her thighs, pumping his fingers in and out while simultaneously playing with her swollen clit. It didn't take much longer before she exploded. Head swimming, her mouth fell open as she stared at the ceiling and the passionate tide overtook her. Air left her lungs in short, harsh gasps, and she sank her nails into his arm as if hanging on for dear life.

Coming down off her high, she saw Reginald slip off the

bed and then return with a couple of condoms. He sheathed himself in protection and kneeled between her open legs.

He gazed down at her with adoration and wonder. "I need to tell you something," he said.

"What?"

He lowered to his forearms above her. "I had the biggest crush on you back in college."

Her eyes widened. "I had no idea."

"If I could have, I would've taken you away from Byron in a second. I guess I told you that because I can't believe you're here, in my bed."

"I have to tell you something too. I had a crush on you back in college, but I never thought you'd be interested in me," she whispered.

"Why not?"

"Because you had so many women. Because you were the Green-Eyed Bandit."

"If I had known, I promise you I would have made a move." A fierceness came into his eyes as he took his length in hand. "Byron would've never stood a chance."

He placed his erection at the entrance of her body and glided into her slick heat. Wet and warm, she readily absorbed his thrust. The pleasure was excruciating and almost unbearable. She lifted her legs around his hips and wound her arms around his neck.

As he moved, she moved with him, and the tips of her breasts dragged against the fine hairs on his chest. He pulled out and eased back, his hips undulating, his eyes locked on hers while the sexy rhythm made her wetter.

Lorna could feel herself losing control. The tension at the base of her spine tightening, she rocked faster against him. His warm breath teased her lips as he continued to ply her with sensual, open-mouthed kisses.

She sensed when he was getting close. His hips accelerated

their movement, and he could no longer kiss her. Instead, he gripped her wrists and held them down on either side of her head.

"Yes, yes, yes," Lorna chanted.

On the cusp of release, she tightened her muscles, and he released the groan of a man near the edge. She teased them with a swift bite to his neck, and he retaliated by angling his hips in such a way that he penetrated deeper and shattered what little control she had left.

Lorna came with a sharp cry, legs clamped around him as she rode out the storm.

"I'm coming," Reginald groaned.

And with that, his body pummeled hers. The bed groaned under the weight of the mighty pumps he used to expel the taut need for release.

When it was all over, he collapsed on top of her and then rolled onto his back. They both lay there for several minutes before she spoke.

"That was incredible. Thank you. It's been a while."

Reginald rolled onto his side and faced her. With gentle fingers, he pushed the damp hair from her forehead.

"Thank *you*," he said. "For giving me another chance."

He gave her a quick kiss and then went to dispose of the condom in the bathroom. When he returned, Reginald pulled her close, and they snuggled under the covers.

She was unable to move because of the muscular arms that held her trapped against his body, but she didn't mind. She was comfortable and content in a way she hadn't been in a very long time.

13

L orna awoke slowly, stretching her limbs under the soft sheets, alone in Reginald's bed. The charcoal floor-length curtains kept out much of the light, but enough filtered in for her to conduct a thorough examination of the room.

The austere lines didn't seem as rigid as the night before. There was almost a comfort in the simplicity of the color scheme. She might add a bit more color here and there, but overall, she felt comforted in the room of grays. The sheets tangled around her limbs were sage and dove gray, and she noted greens and tans in the abstract paintings on the wall.

The wide bed, low to the floor, was comfortable and offered plenty of support while Reginald thrust his body into hers, bringing her to orgasm twice in one night before sleep claimed them. She bit her bottom lip, her lady parts tingling and her toes curling at the memories.

Her eyes landed on the digital clock on the table across the room, and she bolted into a sitting position. *Shoot.* She had a two o'clock vow renewal, and it was already after eleven. She needed to get home, change, and check in with the coordinator handling the ceremony.

Lorna scrambled from the bed and dressed in a hurry, not bothering to tie her scarf around her neck. She went into the adjoining bathroom and splashed water on her face. With her scarf in hand, she exited the bedroom and the scent of cooking food greeted her.

Oh lord, he cooked too. The man was damn near perfect. Even if all he could do was throw together a quick breakfast, it was a nice gesture. One she appreciated but wouldn't have time to indulge in because of the time.

She watched Reginald at the stove for a moment, working in a pair of boxer shorts and an open shirt hanging loosely from his shoulders as he shifted food from the hot pan to a plate.

His home was definitely nice. There was a deck outside, which she hadn't noticed last night. He owned the kind of place perfect for entertaining. She saw him as the entertaining type, and so was she. She could see herself here with him, fixing drinks for their guests and serving hors d'oeuvres as they lingered inside and outside.

Slow down, girl, you're getting ahead of yourself, she thought. Except, was she? She hadn't felt this way in so long. Not since she lost Marcus. This excitement, the elevated blood pressure —all of it seemed brand new in the wake of dating options since his passing.

She embraced the feelings with open arms. Love is a many splendored thing. She'd always believed that—despite her loss —and the way Reginald made her feel confirmed her heart could experience it again.

When she walked over to him, a broad smile broke over his face at the sight of her.

"Hey there, you're up. I'm almost done with breakfast."

He'd made quite an effort—scrambled eggs, sausage links, and waffles from a press on the counter.

"Everything looks delicious, but I can't stay," she said with deep regret.

"What?" His mouth fell open in shock.

"Believe me, I hate having to leave more than you do, but I have a vow renewal today, and I need to get my butt home to shower and change."

His shoulders and face fell in disappointment, making her feel worse.

"I'm so sorry," Lorna said again.

"Well, if you gotta go, you gotta go." He looked at the food as if wondering what he should do with all of it.

She slipped her arms under the open shirt and around his waist and encountered warm skin. "I wish I could stay, but I can't." She kissed his right pec and gazed up at him. "I'll make it up to you."

"You're going to have to. You know, it seems all our times together are to make up a slight or pay each other back for something we've done."

She laughed. "Does seem that way, doesn't it?"

He dropped the spatula and placed his arms around her. "I understand. You gotta work, and I spend a lot of time working on the weekends too. It's the nature of the business, so I'll let you off the hook."

"Thanks. I'm off on Mondays. Want to get together then?" Lorna asked hopefully.

"Yes. Let's do that."

She immediately grinned, excited about the prospect of seeing him again.

"We'll talk later."

She pulled away, but he pulled her back in for a quick kiss. Goodness, his mouth was addictive. She could kiss him for hours.

With a reluctant moan, she eased away, and he chuckled, releasing her.

"I really have to go," she said with deep regret.

Lorna picked up her purse and let him escort her to the front door.

"You better call me when you get finished later today."

"I will, I promise," she said over her shoulder.

She hurried to the car and waved as she backed out the driveway. He waved back, and for the first time ever she wished she didn't have to go to work. She would have loved to linger at Reginald's house the rest of the day.

As she reminisced on the drive home, her phone rang. Tessa.

"Where are you? I've been trying to reach you all morning?"

"Have you? I haven't checked my messages yet," Lorna said.

"Yet? It's almost noon."

"I know. I got a late start this morning."

Pause.

"Should I ask why?"

Lorna slowed to a stop behind an SUV at the light. "You could, but I'm not sure I'd tell you."

"You were with him, weren't you?" Tessa guessed.

Lorna grinned as she pulled off. "Yes."

"Well, well, well, I guess the second date went better?"

"It did. We had a great time. We went to see Eric's work at the gallery, then to dinner, and then dancing."

"Dinner and dancing? Men still do that?"

"Yes, they do."

"You sound happy," Tessa remarked.

"I am." She might be smiling for the rest of the day.

"I'm happy for you. You're not moving too fast though, are you?"

"Absolutely not. In fact, I think he feels the same way I do." She thought about how the barista had called him out at the coffee shop. Though she never mentioned it, she found it interesting that he'd been coming to the shop every day while pretending they had run into each other. "We're seeing each other again on Monday."

"That's wonderful. At some point, I'm going to have to meet this man."

"I'll make sure you do. Maybe I'll bring him to your spring party."

Each April, Tessa invited friends to her home for a party to welcome in the spring and celebrate the renewing of life, as she called it.

"That would be perfect."

"Then it's a date, assuming we're together then." She sincerely hoped they would be. "Now, about this afternoon's event, I'm sure you were calling me for a specific reason. Is there a problem?"

Tessa released an exaggerated sigh. "The mother of the groom is adamant she doesn't want to sit next to her son's father. They're exes and had some kind of falling out, so you need to rearrange the place cards as soon as you get to the venue."

"Got it."

"Also, the florist is short staffed. The wife changed her mind about the bouquet at the last minute, but they don't have anyone who can deliver the new flowers. The shop is near your apartment. Any chance you could swing by and pick it up before you go to the venue?"

"Don't worry, I'll take care of it."

"I knew I could count on you." Tessa let out an audible sigh of relief.

"I'm almost home. I'll take care of everything. Enjoy your day off."

"Thank you, my dear. I'll see you Tuesday."

Lorna hung up and made the rest of the drive in silence.

She itched to send a message to Reginald but held off because she didn't want to seem too eager.

When she arrived at home, she took a quick shower and changed into a green pantsuit and brushed her hair into smooth lines that cradled her head. A little bit of makeup and she was ready to go.

As she slid into the car on the way to the florist, her phone beeped. It was a message from Reginald.

Thinking about you. Have a good day.

Lorna smiled and texted him back.

Thank you. You too.

She paused, then typed what was on her mind.

Can't wait to see you Monday.

Until Monday, he responded.

14

"Who is this? Could you please put Reggie on the phone?" Xavier's sarcastic voice came through the Jaguar's speakers.

Reginald laughed at his cousin's theatrics. "You done?"

"I'm not sure. I honestly can't believe you're spending this much time with a woman, *and* you're talking about it," Xavier said.

He chuckled at the alarm in his cousin's voice. "I like her, man."

Reginald had told Xavier about how he and Lorna spent the last two and a half weeks. Neither of them could cook very well, so they met each night for dinner at a different restaurant or ordered in and stayed at his house.

The first week, they had met on her day off, Monday, as planned. What Reginald didn't tell his cousin was that his days off were now Mondays as well, so they could have more time together.

This past Monday he gave Lorna a guest pass to the gym so she could join him as he trained for the Grady Baby race next week. She had already switched with a co-worker and would be off on Saturday to support him.

When he finished training, they went for lunch and then to the grocery store because as they talked over their meals, she discovered he liked pineapple upside down cake and was determined to show him she could make a delicious one. She loved to bake—one of the many things he discovered while spending time with her. Every time they talked or saw each other, there was a new revelation that made him want to learn more.

During the last week and a half, Lorna made three cakes. The pineapple upside down cake, a lemon pound cake, and a chocolate cake. All were delicious. At this point, he was ready to give her a key to his home based on her baking skills alone.

"She's different from me, and I enjoy every minute I'm with her," Reginald continued. "Last weekend we went dancing again, and Monday afternoon we went to an estate sale, and she bought a music box. You know what's crazy? I didn't mind spending over two hours at that place and only walking out with one item. She was excited by her find, and I was happy to be with her."

To his own ears, that sounded crazy and corny and completely out of character.

Xavier let out a surprised whistle. "This sounds pretty serious."

"I don't know if it's serious, but it's strange."

Strange in a good way. Strange in a way that made him rethink his priorities and reservations about relationships.

"I have to tell Chase what you've told me. He'll never believe me."

Traffic slowed to a crawl and Reginald guarded the brakes with his foot. "I don't believe it myself."

He would never admit this out loud, but when he and Lorna weren't together, he thought about her all the time. Work was a nuisance. At this point, there was no other explanation. The woman had him sprung.

"If I didn't know better, I'd say you were falling in love," Xavier said.

Reginald snorted. "Let's not get carried away, okay? Not counting college, we haven't known each other that long. I'm having a good time and like being with her, and we'll leave it at that."

"If you say so," Xavier said, his voice infused with skepticism. "Are you bringing her to Sunday dinner any time soon?"

Once a month they met at Chase's parents' house for Sunday dinner. Other than Bria, he had never brought a woman to any of their get-togethers.

"Too soon for that, Zay," he said.

"If you say so."

"What's up with you and Zena? By the way, I enjoyed the concert last weekend. That girl can blow."

Zena was a legal assistant and aspiring singer Xavier had recently become involved with. Oddly enough, now that he thought about it, he and his three cousins had all recently met women they were serious about.

"I'm really feeling her, and it kind of hit me out of the blue. Yeah, I know you probably think it's too soon, but I'm thirty-five, not-twenty-five, and I know what I want."

"I'm not judging," Reginald said.

"That's a shock," Xavier said.

"My thoughts on relationships are evolving,"

"That's good to hear," Xavier said with a laugh. "Listen, I better run and get back to work."

"All right, talk to you later."

Reginald hung up and immediately wanted to call Lorna, but she was at work, and he'd already texted her this morning. He needed to chill or he'd chase her away. Women didn't like men who were too into them, and he himself always saw needy behavior as a sign of weakness.

He spent the rest of the day dealing with work issues. He fielded calls from vendors interested in getting on his preferred vendor list and called a customer who was dissatisfied with his party. The man had picked the lowest tier package but somehow expected the full VIP treatment.

Around eleven thirty, Reginald stopped working and got an idea. He wanted to take Lorna lunch. She had enjoyed the macaroni and cheese at Soul Kitchen. Maybe he should surprise her.

He rocked back and forth in his squeaky leather chair and contemplated the decision. Would the gesture be too much? He liked giving women gifts, but spontaneously showing up with lunch was definitely new. What the hell. He was doing it.

He pushed back his chair, exited his office, and stopped at the desk of his office manager. "I'll be back in a couple of hours," he told her.

"Client meeting?" she asked.

"Nah, something personal. Call my cell if you need me."

"Will do," she said, and he was out the door.

He called in the orders on the way to the restaurant. He ordered the roasted chicken, macaroni and cheese, and steamed carrots for both of them, but ordered an extra side of mac and cheese for himself. On the way to the restaurant, he stopped at a flower shop and purchased a small bouquet.

By the time he had picked up the food and was on his way to Crosby Nuptials, he began to reconsider. He and Lorna weren't supposed to get together again until tomorrow night because she had a vow renewal ceremony tonight. But he needed his Lorna fix and didn't want to wait until tomorrow before he saw her again.

"Oh well, too late now," Reginald muttered to himself as he pulled in front of her workplace.

He gathered up his purchases and went inside. He greeted the woman at the desk. "I'm here to see Lorna Kessler," he said.

She eyed him with cool curiosity. "Is she expecting you?"

"No, actually, it's a surprise. My name is Reggie Knight. I brought her lunch." He held up the bag of food.

She looked at the food and the flowers, and the corners of her lips tipped up slightly in approval. "One moment please."

Her voice had sweetened, which confirmed he had made the right decision, and he couldn't wait to see Lorna's expression.

She made a call to the back, and after a brief conversation, hung up. "She'll be right out."

"Thank you."

While he waited, Reginald strolled across the floor to look at the photographs of smiling couples on the wall. Some were weddings, but most were obviously vow renewals. They didn't have the formality of a wedding ceremony, with the groomsmen and bridesmaids or the formal dress and veil. One appeared to be in someone's backyard. Another one, outside, made him step closer for an inspection. He recognized the man in the photo as former Atlanta Braves baseball player, Damon Foster.

"Hey."

He heard Lorna's soft voice behind him and turned around. As always, her friendly brown eyes and striking features punched him in the gut. He was glad he came.

She had her bag over her shoulder, so she was clearly ready for lunch.

"Hey." He angled his chin at the photos on the wall. "Is that Damon 'The Flash' Foster?" he asked.

She nodded. "Last summer he hired us to coordinate a vow renewal for him and his wife. The publicity changed the trajectory of our business." She glanced at the bag and flowers in his hand, and a smile broke out on her face. "What's this?"

"These are for you." He handed her the flowers.

Lorna's smile widened, and she brought them to her nose. "These are beautiful."

"They made me think of you, so I had to get them."

"Thank you." Her cheeks reddened as she blushed.

He held up the bag of food. "This is lunch from Soul Kitchen."

Her eyes widened. "Don't tell me there's macaroni and cheese in there."

"There's macaroni and cheese in here."

She groaned. "Oh gosh, I didn't know you were coming. This is such a nice surprise, but I can't join you." Deep regret filled her voice.

Reginald's shoulders slumped in disappointment. "You already have plans?"

"I do. I'm...." Her voice trailed off as the door behind her opened, and in walked Eric McBride.

He wore a different pair of glasses from the black ones Reginald had originally seen him in. This pair was gold-framed.

Reginald's attitude immediately soured. Eric smiled at them both, but Reginald could almost swear he saw a challenge in the other man's eyes.

Straightening the glasses on his face, Eric waved at Drea.

She waved back. "Hi, Eric."

Eric walked over and extended his hand to Reginald. "Good to see you again. Are you joining us for lunch?" He didn't sound enthusiastic.

Lorna answered before Reginald could. "Actually, he brought me lunch. It was a surprise."

"Oh, that's too bad, because I'm taking our girl to eat. It's something we do every so often."

Eric threw an arm around Lorna's shoulders.

Reginald's eyes darted to Lorna's shoulder before returning

to Eric's face. He really wanted to punch this guy. "I'll have to catch *my girl* another time, I guess," he said.

Eric frowned.

"We're still on for tomorrow night, right?" Lorna asked.

"Yes. I'll see you tomorrow night."

"Thank you for the beautiful flowers and lunch. If I'd known..."

"Don't worry about it. If you'd known, it wouldn't be a surprise. We can have these meals for dinner when you come over tomorrow night."

"Good plan." Her eyes searched his face, but he kept his expression neutral. He didn't want to act like a jealous fool in front of her, but more importantly, he didn't want Eric to know he was jealous of him.

They walked out of the building together. Reginald carried the food he bought and had to watch Eric open the passenger door of his sedan and let Lorna slide into the seat with the flowers he'd bought her.

Inside his own vehicle, Reginald pretended to be busy with the dashboard, but he really wanted them to leave first, which they did.

As he pulled out of the lot, he tried to convince himself that he was overreacting. There was nothing going on between Eric and Lorna. But the more he thought about their "every so often" lunch dates, the more doubts he had about Eric's intentions.

Lorna might not be interested in Eric and might only see him as a good friend.

But Eric... that man was definitely interested in her.

15

W hen the doorbell rang, Reginald already knew it was Lorna. She called ahead to let him know she was on her way. When he opened the door, she stood on the doorstep holding a plate covered with aluminum foil.

"Hi," he said in a neutral voice, purposely tamping down the excitement at seeing her. He was still smarting from watching her go off with Eric the day before.

He peered over her shoulder, and she glanced behind her to see what he was watching.

"What are you looking at?" she asked.

"I'm checking for your shadow," Reginald answered.

She rolled her eyes. "Can I come in?"

"Depends. What's in your hand?"

She smiled sweetly and held the plate higher. "Pineapple upside down cake. Your favorite."

His mouth watered at the prospect of cutting into a slice of her moist, delicious cake, but he remained rigid and unmoving. "You can't bribe me with cake."

Her eyes narrowed. "I can't? That's too bad. I guess I'll leave then."

She turned to go, but Reginald quickly grabbed her around the waist and pulled her against him. The cushion of her soft ass butted up against his pelvis.

"You're not going anywhere." He growled and kissed her neck. Then he pulled her into the apartment.

"Help. I'm being kidnapped," Lorna whisper-yelled, laughing as he shut the door behind them. She spun to face him. "I knew this would get me through the door."

Reginald frowned at her with mock anger. "You're a calculating woman."

With a smug expression, she walked with extra swagger toward the kitchen, moving through his home with the familiarity of frequent visits. She took a knife from one of the drawers and a small plate from out of a cabinet.

"When did you have time to bake?"

"I left work a little early today since I oversaw the ceremony last night."

When she removed the aluminum foil, he saw she'd brought half a cake.

"Where's the rest of it?"

"Don't be greedy. I'm taking the other half to work to share with my colleagues, if that's all right with you." She cut off a hunk of cake and slid it over to him with a fork. "Peace offering."

"You would only need a peace offering if you did something wrong. Did you do something wrong?"

"No, but I know you weren't pleased when you saw Eric yesterday."

Reginald snorted. "Gee, what gave me away?"

Lorna pursed her lips. "He's a nice guy."

"So you've told me." He ate a piece of cake, and once again it was outrageously good. Moist and sweet and taking him back to his childhood when his grandmother—his father's mother—lived a couple of doors down. She always had a freshly baked cake or pie for when family or friends visited.

He could well imagine Lorna being the same way. He and she might have a couple of children of their own, and she'd serve her delicious baked goods to the neighborhood kids or friends and family when they came to visit. They'd need a bigger house than the one he owned now, but—*whoa*.

He and Lorna hadn't been together very long as a couple. Only a couple of months. It was way too soon to be having those types of thoughts. He didn't *have* those types of thoughts.

Yet, he could absolutely see her as the mother of his kids. They'd have two, maybe three. And she'd be a great mother too. No doubt about it.

"I talked to Eric," Lorna said.

Reginald cut another piece of cake. "About what?"

"About his feelings for me."

His eyebrows shot skyward.

"I know you think he might have a little crush on me," she continued.

"A little?"

She folded her arms over her chest and ignored his comment. He liked when she got saucy.

"*Anyway*, I decided to ask him directly about his feelings. We have that kind of relationship, where we can talk about anything. He denied having feelings for me. I pressed him on the subject, and he continued to deny it."

"And you believe him?"

"There's no reason not to," Lorna said. "There's a certain amount of trust needed in all relationships—including friendships."

"I agree with you, but I don't believe he told you the truth."

"Based on the conversation we had, I believe he did."

"You're too trusting. Tell me again why the two of you didn't work out?"

"I knew he wasn't the right man for me," Lorna said simply with a shrug.

"How did you know that?"

Her lips shifted into a moue as she fell into deep thought. Dang, she was adorable. Reginald had to concentrate on the conversation and resist kissing her puckered lips. In the silence, he continued to eat the tasty cake.

"Eric is a great person, but being a great person doesn't mean he's the right man for me. I guess I knew he wasn't the right one because I've been in love before. I told you that I lost my fiancé, Marcus. I knew what being in love with him felt like, and I didn't experience the same emotions with Eric. I recognized the difference and was honest. Your suspicions about him made me wonder if I had missed the signs of interest, but I didn't, so now you can stop worrying."

"Who said I was worried?"

Lorna moved closer and tilted her head to the side. "I know you were. Your eyes get darker when you're fighting back emotion."

Reginald arched an eyebrow. "Oh really? I need to figure out how to control that."

"You can't. It's involuntary, and very noticeable when you're on top of me."

His mouth went dry. "Oh yeah?"

"Yes," she said.

Reginald abandoned the last piece of cake and stepped into her personal space, forcing her head to tilt backward so they could maintain eye contact. The alluring scent of her perfume filled his nostrils. Without saying a word, he looped an arm around her waist and drew her against his body.

Their kiss was slow and exploratory, as if they were kissing for the first time. Already his body was awakening to the sensation of *her* body against his. Soft. Feminine.

He lifted his other hand to her nape and deepened the kiss. Slipping her some tongue, he grabbed one butt cheek and took pleasure in the sound of her low moan.

Lorna curled her fingers into the front of his shirt. "I thought you were mad at me," she whispered, biting her bottom lip.

"I was, for about one whole second. I don't think I can stay mad at you," Reginald said in a low, gravelly voice.

"That's a good thing," she whispered.

Before he could respond, her lids lowered over her eyes, her lips parted in a tempting invitation, and he kissed her again—harder this time.

She leaned into him and wrapped her arms around his torso, causing him to experience the full length of her body. Firm thighs, soft belly and even softer breasts.

Reluctantly, Reginald lifted his head and broke the kiss. "I have dinner from Soul Kitchen in the fridge. I know you must be hungry." He whispered the words halfheartedly against the arch of her throat. He had promised to feed her, but his mind was elsewhere at the moment.

"Forget about dinner for now. I'm hungry for something completely different. You."

His pulse kicked into overdrive. Damn, he loved her honesty. No beating around the bush. No playing coy.

They may not agree on everything, but they certainly thought the same when it counted. Right now, they both wanted sex.

"I'm the kind of man who likes to give a woman what she wants."

With a slick smile, Reginald lifted her from the floor and cradled her bottom with his hands. Her arms curled around his neck.

Nothing else mattered in that moment. One would think they hadn't made love only days ago, but his thirst for Lorna remained unquenchable. Strolling through the house, they indulged in a tasty, wet kiss that communicated how much he wanted her, and how much she wanted him.

With their mouths seared together and her legs wrapped around his waist, they entered his bedroom for pre-dinner lovemaking.

16

E arly Saturday morning, Lorna was standing on Holland Farms, a more than five thousand-acre property located a short distance outside the city of Atlanta. Participants came from all over the metro area to raise funds for Grady Hospital's neonatal unit.

The event included a bike race, runners—of which Reginald was one of many—and walkers.

In addition to the contestants and spectators, medical personnel were on site offering health screenings, answering questions about pregnancy, childcare, and various illnesses. Vendors sold food and beverages at covered tables, and in general people milled around enjoying the morning before the sun came out in full force.

Lorna stood on the sidelines in sunglasses, shorts, and a wide-brimmed hat. Reginald was among the other contestants, but he wasn't paying her any attention. He was in the zone, in the middle of stretching exercises to prepare for the run.

She was proud of him. He was one of the top fundraisers, having raised over $10,000 in sponsorships. She pulled in some dollars for him herself, hitting up Tessa and a few of the employees on the job.

Reginald scanned the crowd, obviously looking for her.

"I'm over here," Lorna called out, waving her hands in the air.

He spotted her and smiled and waved back. Then he became focused again, staring at the track ahead. When the time for the race to start grew near, the runners lined up, the announcer fired a gun, and they took off.

The more than six-mile course consisted of running along a paved road for a short period and then moving onto the grassy areas. The course took them alongside a lake, which they would round and then come back toward the finish line. Water stops along the way helped them stay hydrated.

"Who are you here with?" a dark haired woman beside her asked. She held a baby in a carrier against her chest.

"My boyfriend. How about you?"

"My husband. He's a doctor and runs multiple events a year, but this is the one that he never misses because it raises funds for where he works."

"Reggie, that's my boyfriend, he runs multiple events a year as well. He used to run track in high school. This is a way for him to stay in shape and continue doing something that he loves."

"That's wonderful. I wasn't sure I'd be able to come today, but this little guy has been an absolute angel since yesterday, and I decided to take a chance."

Lorna looked at the sleeping baby. "How old is he?"

"Almost six months."

"First one?"

The woman nodded. "Do you have any of your own?"

"No, but I hope to one day."

"I never wanted to be a mother for the longest, but then one day I up and decided I didn't want to let the opportunity pass me by. I told my husband I had changed my mind, and lucky for me, he was on board. So we had a baby!" She laughed, as if she couldn't believe they had done something so crazy. "He'll probably be the only one, but I don't regret it. I can't wait to see the person he becomes."

Envy nipped at the outskirts of Lorna's brain. She hoped one day to have children of her own. At thirty-five, she worried that time was slipping away from her. She and Reginald talked about all kinds of topics, but oddly enough, they had never touched on whether they wanted kids.

Did he want children? And how many?

Perhaps that was a topic she could broach with him soon.

"My name is Sally," the woman said, extending a hand.

"Lorna. Nice to meet you."

They kept each other company for the rest of the race. Lorna learned that Sally was a nurse and had taken a leave of absence to spend as much time as possible with her son. When she learned Lorna coordinated vow renewals, she expressed interest in a ceremony for her and her husband.

Lorna pulled out a business card. "Whenever you're ready, give me a call. I'll walk you through the options based on your budget. Vow renewals are typically less expensive than a wedding, but you can have a beautiful event. They can be as simple or extravagant as you like. It's completely up to you."

"Wonderful. I'll have to mention it to my husband. Our tenth anniversary is around the corner."

Less than forty minutes later, the racers bounded toward them. When Lorna saw Reginald near the front, she became excited. There were three people ahead of him, but his speed increased, and he cut the distance between them as they neared the finish line.

"Come on, Reggie!" Lorna hollered.

"Which one is your guy?" Sally asked.

"Number forty-seven."

"Come on, Reggie!" Sally screamed.

The other spectators hollered and clapped for the incoming racers. When Reginald cruised past the third in line, a cry of excitement went up from the crowd.

"Come on! Come on!" Lorna and Sally yelled.

Lorna bounced up and down as Reginald neared the woman in second place.

"He might actually be able to win this thing," she whispered to herself.

She jumped up and down like a high school cheerleader, hollering as if the sound of her voice could propel him to the front of the line. Maybe it worked. The next thing she knew, he passed the woman in second place, and he and the first place runner were neck and neck.

They both wore grimaces of effort as they pushed their bodies to the limit toward the finish line. Lorna didn't know the other man's background but believed Reggie's experience would help him. Sure enough, he pulled ahead and leaned across the finish line.

First place!

"He did it!" Sally sounded excited, as if she knew Reginald personally.

Lorna cheered with the rest of the spectators at the photo finish. Reginald slowed to a stop and rested his hands on his knees. Panting hard, he looked over to where she jumped up and down and grinned.

"Yay!" She blew kisses at him as people crowded around and congratulated him.

Sally's husband came through at number fifteen, and Lorna helped cheer him across the finish line as well.

Officials gave the top three finishers medallions to hang around their necks and lots of photos were taken by the local news and the event photographers. Much later, Reginald jogged over, and Lorna flung her arms around him.

He chuckled. "I stink, baby."

"I don't care." She gripped his face and gave him a big kiss. "Congratulations. I'm so proud of you."

He gave her a quick squeeze before letting go.

Lorna introduced him to Sally, who in turn introduced them to her husband when he came over.

"You two did amazing. I could never run for that long of a period," Lorna said.

"It's fun," Sally's husband said. He had dark brown hair and a friendly smile.

"Next time I'm getting you to run with me," Reginald told Lorna.

"No way, but I'll always be around to cheer you on."

A knot formed in her stomach when she thought of them being together months from now. Years from now.

She wanted to tell him the depths of her feelings and let him know how incredible the past couple of months with him had been. She was falling in love with him. She might already be in love with him.

"Uh-oh, he's awake," Sally said, gazing down at her son, who looked around in confusion.

"Poor thing, he's probably wondering who all these people are." Lorna bent her head to the little boy. "Hey, sweetie, how are you? Did you have a good nap? I'm Lorna, and this is Reggie."

The little boy blinked at her, and then his face cleared, and he blessed her with a toothless grin.

Sally and her husband laughed.

"Aw, look at that smile," Lorna said, glancing back at Reginald.

He wasn't looking at the baby. He was looking at her. When their eyes met, she couldn't read his expression, but he wasn't smiling.

"I'm gonna get some water. You want one?" Reginald asked.

"Yes, please."

He strolled toward one of the food and beverage stands, and she continued to play with the baby. Her mind raced with a million thoughts, ruminating on Reginald's cool reaction to the child. She recalled his comments about his ex's desire to have children. Did he not want kids?

Lorna continued chatting with Sally and her husband and played with their son. There was no sound as beautiful as a baby's laugh. When Reginald returned with the water, she took a bottle from him.

Sally and her husband said goodbye, but Lorna and Reginald stayed long enough to see the cyclists return after they completed their course. The winner in that race was a woman in her sixties who, according to Reginald, had won the race the year before too.

"Age ain't nothing but a number for real," Lorna murmured as they walked away.

They strolled to the parking lot where Reginald had parked his Jaguar.

Lorna slid into the car and buckled her seat belt. "Chatting with Sally was nice," she said.

"She and her husband seem like good people," Reginald commented, starting the car.

"While you were running, she told me that was their first baby. She didn't want kids at first but changed her mind."

"Happens to a lot of people. I guess sometimes you meet the right person and they can make you change your mind. Of course, the wrong person can make you go the other way too."

Lorna let out a little laugh. "True."

She fell silent, wondering how to broach the topic that she wanted to. She decided to just do it. She could be honest and forthright with Reginald.

"You seemed sort of standoffish back there. How do you feel about children?"

"I like them." He glanced at her with a frown.

"Maybe I misread your reaction. You seemed a little detached."

"You definitely misread me."

"So... you can see yourself as a father one day?"

"One day. Eventually."

She relaxed. He didn't come across as excited about the topic, but he didn't seem averse, either, as she'd originally thought.

"How many children do you think you'd like to have?"

He glanced at her and smiled. "Where are all these questions coming from?"

"Just wondering." Had she gone too far?

"What was the question again?"

"How many children would you like to have?"

"Two. Maybe three. And you?"

"Same," Lorna answered, but the enthusiasm she had for the topic was tempered.

Talking to Reginald about the number of kids they wanted made her feel as if she were intruding into his personal life, when in fact that shouldn't be the case. They should be able to talk easily and comfortably about the topic. They'd known each other long enough and spent a lot of time together. They should be able to have these types of conversations without awkwardness—assuming they had a future together.

Was that the problem? They had no future together?

Her heart jump-started, and she watched Reginald from the corner of her eye. Were they on the same page regarding their relationship?

"What do you want for lunch?" he asked.

"I'm open. Whatever you choose is fine."

"How about we go by my place so I can take a quick shower, and then we can go somewhere to eat. I'm in the mood for Mexican food. That sound good to you?"

"Perfect," Lorna said in an upbeat tone, though she felt anything but upbeat.

Why did Reginald seem hesitant to talk to her about his desire for children? More importantly, she saw a future with Reginald. But did he see a future with *her*?

17

H e couldn't breathe with the pillow over his face. His mouth fell open to suck in air, but that didn't work. His mouth became stuck, wide open as if in a silent scream, and not a single molecule of air made its way into his lungs. His hands thrashed about. He was going to black out. He was going to die.

Reginald sat up with a jolt and sucked air into his lungs. The sound of his heavy breathing filled the darkness of the room, and when a gentle hand touched his shoulder, he jumped.

It was Lorna.

"Are you okay?" she asked.

One hand curled into the rumpled bed sheets, and he wiped sweat from his brow. He still had a hard time breathing, but it became easier as his heart rate slowed to a normal cadence.

He shook off the dizzying effect of the lack of oxygen. Despite only being a dream, his body reacted as if someone had really held a pillow over his face.

"Yes, I'm fine," he managed.

He swung his legs over the side of the mattress and sat there for a while.

"You were tossing in your sleep, but I was afraid to wake you. That was quite a dream."

After half a night's sleep, Lorna's voice sounded husky, but along with her gentle touch, it soothed him in the darkness.

"More like a nightmare."

"Do you remember it?"

Reginald paused as bits and pieces came back. "No," he lied.

He massaged the back of his neck to ease the throbbing headache at the base of his skull. He didn't know how to explain what he remembered. *Lorna* had placed the pillow over his face. She had attacked him. What did the dream mean?

Pushing off the bed, Reginald padded into the adjoining bathroom. He flipped on the light and squinted against the sudden glare. Taking a bottle of ibuprofen from the medicine cabinet, he popped a couple in his mouth and used water from the faucet to wash them down.

He splashed water on his face and stared at his bleary-eyed reflection. That had been intense.

Lorna came to stand in the doorway and watched him with concerned eyes. He had given her a faded blue T-shirt to sleep in, and it looked way better on her than it ever did on him. With her rumpled short hair and face makeup free, she was sexy as sin, but right now the last thing he wanted to do was get between her legs.

He couldn't understand why he dreamed about her trying to kill him. He'd never seen her act in a violent way, and she'd never raised her voice the entire time they'd been together.

"You look worried, but I'm fine. It was only a bad dream," he said to ease the worry lines in her forehead.

"A nightmare," she corrected, using his words from before.

"Yes."

"Has this ever happened to you before?"

"No. Never had a dream like that." At least that part was true.

He turned off the light, edged past her, and climbed into bed. She came toward him slowly and hovered nearby.

"Stop worrying," Reginald chided.

"I can't help but worry. I care about you."

"Come on, get in the bed." He patted the spot beside him.

Lorna climbed under the covers with him, and he pulled her close. They hadn't been cuddling when he woke up, but he needed to hold her right now.

She didn't seem to mind, resting her head on his shoulder and placing one smooth leg across his.

"Reggie?"

"Hmm?"

"You sure you don't remember what you were dreaming about?"

"I'm sure."

She remained quiet for a moment, but the tension in her body belied that she wasn't completely satisfied with the answer.

"It sounded like you said my name," she whispered.

Three seconds ticked by before he answered.

"I'm sure you misunderstood."

She lifted her head and looked at him. He didn't avert his gaze.

She smiled. "You're right. Must have been something else I heard. Good night." She placed her head on his shoulder again.

Reginald breathed easier, but it took a while for him to fall asleep.

Why had he dreamt that Lorna was trying to kill him?

~

LORNA STEPPED out of Reginald's front door. He was washing her car in the driveway with his muscular legs on display in a pair of basketball shorts. Water dripped from his Jaguar, which he had washed first.

After a late breakfast, he had come outside to take care of the cars. A hose lay beside him on the wet pavement. As he washed her car, his firm biceps contracted and relaxed for all the world to see in a shirt with the sleeves cut off.

"Do you want me to order lunch?" she asked.

He looked up from his chore. "That sounds good. I'll be done in a little bit. I want to clean the inside of your car after I get finished with the outside." He looked pointedly at her.

Lorna didn't think her car was in such bad shape. Granted, she hadn't washed it in a while, but Reginald acted as if she was driving a toxic waste dump. She had to admit though, it was nice to have him take over this particular task because it wasn't exactly a priority for her.

She shrugged. "I haven't had time to clean the car. Don't judge me."

"I checked your oil too. When was the last time you had it changed?"

That had to be a trick question. The look on his face clearly indicated he knew she hadn't changed her oil in a long time.

"Huh?"

"You heard me, Lorna. When was the last time you had your oil changed?"

"Honestly, I can't remember," she said lamely.

"You need to change your oil regularly. You don't have to do it as often as back in the day, but it's necessary to keep your engine clean and help it run more efficiently."

"That's just the mechanic industry trying to get you to spend more money on oil changes. It's a racket."

Reginald laughed as he turned on the water and started

washing away the suds. "It's not a racket, sweetheart. You can end up with major problems without regular oil changes."

"Fine, I'll take the car for an oil change tomorrow on my day off."

"I'll change the oil for you myself tomorrow. I'm doing mine, so I'll do yours. In the morning I'll run by the auto parts store and get the oil and filter. From now on, your car is on the same maintenance schedule my car is on." Even when he was giving her a hard time, he was sweet.

"You don't have to do that," Lorna said.

Reginald glanced back at her. "You think I'm going to let you drive around in a poorly maintained car while mine is in tip top shape? I'm also going to take it to my mechanic for a once over because I have a funny feeling your lackluster approach to taking care of your vehicle could be hiding other problems."

"I do care about the car, it's just not a priority, I guess. Thank you."

"Think about all the things this car does for you. Takes you to lunch. Takes you to work. Takes you home. Brings you to me. We gotta make sure we take care of it."

"I don't need a lecture. I *said* thank you."

Reginald shot her another look. "Are you getting smart with me?"

"Maybe."

She smirked at him, and he narrowed his eyes. Without warning, he swung the hose toward her.

Lorna screeched and scampered toward the front door.

She frowned at her damp shirt and shorts. "You're so mean. You didn't have to wet me up."

"That's what you get for having a smart mouth. Now order me lunch, woman," Reginald said over his shoulder.

"I should let you starve," she mumbled.

"What was that?"

"I said, right away, sir," Lorna said.

Their eyes met and from his smile, he knew she was lying. She couldn't help the smile that came to her face too.

Moments like this reminded her of how compatible she and Reginald were. Whenever they were in each other's company, their playfulness and the laughter they shared filled her with happiness. She hated having to return to her apartment after spending time with him.

Perhaps yesterday with the baby was simply an odd moment for Reginald. Perhaps she was overthinking his reaction because she remembered what he had said about his ex that night in Decatur.

She harassed me about kids.

But she wasn't his ex, and she wasn't a nag. She simply wanted to know that she and Reginald had a future together, and right now she believed that was possible. He had done so much to show her.

They had the same days off, and minutes ago he added maintenance of her vehicle into the scheduled maintenance of his. Every day, he gave her signs that she had made the right decision by accepting him into her life.

And every day she fell more in love with him.

18

When Reginald arrived at home, Lorna came out of his house in a flowing maxi dress, looking like she stepped out the pages of a magazine. He was a lucky man.

After a quick kiss, she gave him Tessa's address, and they took off to the destination. The spring weather was perfect—not hot or cold—just right for an afternoon barbecue with friends.

Her boss's home was located south of Atlanta in a gated community filled with brick houses of various sizes. Cars filled the driveway and lined the street.

"How many people are here?" Reginald asked as he pulled in front of the house.

"There'll be up to fifty or so people once the party really gets started. They're people from work and some of Tessa's personal family and friends."

They stepped out of the car, and Reginald placed a hand at the small of Lorna's back. The front door opened, and a woman with graying natural hair and glasses stood before them in a colorful top and jeans.

She gave Lorna a hug and then stretched out a hand to Reginald. "You must be Reggie. Nice to meet you."

He gave her hand a firm clasp. "Nice to meet you too."

"Come on in. Everyone is in the back."

She led them through a tastefully decorated house, across tiled floors and into an open kitchen where French doors led to a tiered backyard. Outside, guests were already gathered around tables eating hot dogs and hamburgers and drinking beer and soda, and low music played in the background.

"Reggie, that's my brother-in-law, Dennis." Tessa pointed to a burly man holding a metal spatula and squinting at the heat coming off the grill. "If you have any special requests—for example, if you want your hot dog or chicken burnt—let him know, and he'll hook you up."

"I'll keep that in mind," Reginald said.

"Help yourselves. Lorna, you've been here before so you know what to do."

"I sure do." She looped an arm through his. "Let me introduce you to a few people."

As more guests arrived, Tessa placed a sign on the door so they could come around to the backyard instead of ringing the doorbell and having to walk through the house.

One of those people was Eric McBride. Inwardly, Reginald groaned.

Him again. Unbelievable.

He and Lorna stood near the fence watching a game of cornhole when her friend arrived. Reginald watched him march across the grass with a purposeful stride, and Lorna waved at him to catch his attention.

"I didn't know he was going to be here," Reginald muttered, sipping on a beer.

"He's gotten to know Tessa and some of my other coworkers. Be nice, please."

"I'm nice. Tell *his* ass to be nice," Reginald muttered.

"Hey, there." Eric came over and immediately pulled Lorna into a hug. Then the smile dropped off his face. "Reggie."

"Hey," Reggie returned with an equal lack of enthusiasm.

"I thought you couldn't make it," Lorna said.

"I didn't think I would be able to, but I finished up sooner than expected," Eric said.

"A wealthy businessman commissioned Eric to take photos of him and his friends while on a sports fishing vacation to Costa Rica," Lorna explained.

"I charged him a ridiculous amount, and he didn't bat an eye. I guess I could have gone higher, but I received a nice vacation out of it, so I won't complain."

"Good for you," Reginald said, and meant it.

He didn't care for Eric, but he wasn't a hater. From what he'd seen of his work at the gallery, Eric was an excellent photographer destined for more notoriety.

"Thanks. I see Drea, so I'll go say hi and fix me a plate," Eric said.

As he walked away, Dennis cranked up the music, and the party really got started. A few people started dancing to the old school hits coming through the speakers, and board games, cards, and dominoes appeared on the tables.

"You two interested in playing Taboo? We need another couple," a woman asked.

Reginald and Lorna looked at each other.

"Let's do it," Reginald said.

Hours later, they had come in dead last in Taboo, but were the couple to beat in dominoes, and tied with Tessa and Dennis in the Spades "tournament."

As the sun went down and day segued into night, Reginald sat alone with his back to the table and observed the energetic group. He imagined him and Lorna entertaining guests at his home in a similar manner. He already had a deck with outdoor furniture and could purchase tables and chairs to accommodate additional guests, the way Lorna's boss had done.

Tessa pulled up a chair and sat beside him. "Did Lorna abandon you?"

He laughed shortly. "No, she's in the bathroom."

"Okay. Are you enjoying yourself?"

He understood why Lorna admired and trusted her. She gave off a motherly vibe.

Reginald nodded. "I'm having a great time, though I wouldn't mind a Taboo rematch. That was a massacre."

She chuckled and sipped water from a clear plastic cup. "That game brings out the worst in people. I don't know which is worse—Taboo or Spades."

They looked at each other.

"Spades," they said at the same time, and busted out laughing.

Lorna approached with a napkin filled with potato chips and sat on the other side of Reginald. "What are you two laughing about?"

"We wholeheartedly agreed that Spades is worse than Taboo. It brings out the worst in people," Tessa said.

"Agreed." Lorna extended the chips to Reginald, and he took a couple.

"This is a nice neighborhood," he remarked. "It's a recent development, isn't it?"

Tessa nodded. "They started it three years ago. I moved in a couple of years ago. I used to have these spring parties at my old place too, but this is much nicer, don't you think, Lorna?"

"Definitely. There's more room, which allows you to invite more people."

"Exactly. Bear would have loved it," Tessa said with a wistful note to her voice.

"Bear?" Reginald repeated.

"My husband. He loved a good party. He's deceased," Tessa explained.

"I told you about him. They used to go to the French restaurant we went to in Decatur," Lorna reminded him.

"Oh, right," Reginald said. "I'm sorry for your loss."

"It's been a long time. I've recovered—for the most part—but being without my Bear means taking this road called life alone. Thought I'd have him by my side for a little longer." She looked off into the distance.

"You ever think you'll get married again?" Reginald asked gently. He didn't want to pry, but he was genuinely curious.

"I'd like to, but you know, it's hard to find a person you're compatible with. When you do..." Tessa kissed the tips of her fingers. "Perfection."

"What are you looking for in a mate?" Reginald asked.

"Why?" Tessa asked with a twinkle in her eye.

"I might be able to hook you up. I know a lot of men looking for a good woman."

"Oh right, all those newly divorced men. They might be too raw, honey."

"Good point," Reginald agreed with a nod.

"*But*, if you know of any men in their late fifties to mid-sixties with a good sense of humor and a zest for travel, let me know."

"Got it."

"She doesn't waste a lot of time trying to figure out if a man is the right one for her," Lorna interjected.

"You don't?" Reginald asked with amusement.

"I certainly do not," Tessa replied. "When you know, you know. Right, Lorna?"

"That's right."

Reginald looked from one to the other. "Hold up, is that women's intuition or something?"

Tessa answered. "It's good old-fashioned common sense.

Don't waste time with partners you don't have a future with, and invest in the partners you know will work out."

"Come on, it's not that easy," Reginald said.

"Of course it is," Tessa said with a frown.

"He's cautious." Lorna ate a chip.

Reginald continued. "We like to talk about a sixth sense when it comes to relationships, but the truth is, you can choose wrong because you *think* the person you're with is the right person. I've seen it over and over again. People divorce for all kinds of reasons. They can't agree on kids, jobs, finances, you name it. There are all kinds of reasons for couples splitting up after they claim to have *known* they found the right person."

"And how do you decide if *you've* found the right person?" Tessa asked.

"Personally, I have a vetting process. Are we compatible sexually? Do we have the same wants and desires? We have to be on the same page regarding children, of course. Et cetera, et cetera. We might be good in those areas, but there's still no guarantee the relationship will work. So I implement a waiting period."

"A waiting period?" Tessa repeated.

"Yes. If you wait long enough, the crazy will come out, and then you'll save yourself a lot of trouble."

"I see," Tessa said slowly. Her gaze shifted to Lorna.

Ah shit. That's what he got for being honest.

"You have a very interesting philosophy. I guess we both have our way of handling the screening process, though I hate that phrase. Screening process. Sounds like a job interview." Tessa stood with a groan. "These old bones aren't what they used to be. Reggie, I have enjoyed our conversation, but I need to check on my other guests. Excuse me."

Reginald and Lorna watched the activity around them in silence.

Finally, he turned to her.

"You know what I said doesn't apply to you, right?"

She faced him with a brittle smile. "Of course."

It was the first time she'd lied to him.

19

"Bye. I had a great time as always." Lorna gave Tessa a hug.

"Thank you for coming, and you too," Tessa said to Reginald. "You're part of the family now, so you get a hug."

"I can live with that," Reginald said with a laugh.

Tessa hugged him and they rocked side to side for a spell before she released him.

Most of the guests had already left, including Eric, so they said goodbye to the few remaining people and walked around the side of the house to the front.

The day had gone well, and Reginald seemed to enjoy himself. He fit in with the group, using his natural charisma sprinkled with humor to charm them all.

He opened the door on her side, and Lorna slipped in. Once he was behind the wheel, she asked, "Did you have a good time?"

"I did. You couldn't tell?"

"I thought so, but I wanted to make sure."

Reginald reversed into one of the neighbor's driveway and turned the car around, heading down the street.

Lorna rested her head against the window's cool glass, watching as the cars and buildings whizzed by. They were halfway back to Reginald's house when he placed a hand on her thigh.

"Tired?"

"A little."

She enjoyed his touch, whether they were holding hands, he was touching the small of her back, or resting his hand on her thigh like this. It was nice to be with a man who wasn't afraid of displaying his affection for her or performing considerate acts, like bringing her lunch from Soul Kitchen. They confirmed he thought about her when they weren't together.

She didn't want to spoil their moment together, but the conversation at Tessa's made her wonder once again if they were on the same page relationship-wise.

"We'll be home soon," Reginald said.

Home.

He said the word casually, but the meaning was not lost on her. They spent most of their time at his place, and it had become a central location in their relationship, but it was *his* home, not hers. Deep down, she needed to know if one day it would be hers too. She turned her head to watch the passing scenery.

"Something wrong, sweetheart?"

She shouldn't go there. She shouldn't create issues where there wasn't a problem. Reginald obviously cared about her, and it should be enough. Yet it wasn't. She needed to know that she wasn't wasting her time.

"Do you want to get married?" she asked.

"Yes." His voice was guarded.

She looked at him, and he glanced at her before returning his eyes to the road.

He cursed softly. "This is about the conversation at Tessa's, isn't it?"

"What phase of the vetting process am I in right now? Are you still figuring out if we're compatible, or are we in the waiting period?"

He sighed heavily. "Do you mind holding off so we can have this conversation at the house?"

Lorna folded her arms and stared out the windshield.

By the time they pulled into the garage, she had resigned to being disappointed in his answer. If they were in the compatibility phase, she still had the waiting period. If they were in the waiting period, she didn't know how long that would take. She suspected he could drag his feet for a long time.

They entered the house in silence, and Reginald tossed the keys on the table in the living room.

"Ask me anything you want, and I'll answer," he said.

"Answer the question I asked you in the car." Lorna dropped her purse on the sofa and rested her hands on her hips.

"I'm not sure what part of the vetting process we're in, Lorna. I feel like we're compatible in a lot of ways, but then you go and do something like this."

"Like what? Try to find out if I'm wasting my time or not?"

"You want quick, simple answers. Relationships aren't like that."

"I love you." Afraid of rejection, she held her breath.

Reginald swallowed. "I love you too. I thought that was obvious, but I have questions about you, Lorna."

She experienced a sense of relief at the ease with which he said he loved her, but that last statement betrayed his hesitation about her. "What questions? Ask *me* anything, and I'll answer."

He paced away from her. "This thing with you and Eric doesn't sit right with me. He's hanging around, taking you to lunch, and showing up at parties."

"He's my *friend*."

"You used to fuck him!" Reginald exclaimed.

"This might be hard for you to believe, but men and women can be friends, even after they've had sex."

"You might not have feelings for him, but he wants you."

"You're wrong. I know everything about him, and I know he's not interested in me."

"Yeah, right," Reginald huffed.

"So you don't trust me?"

"I don't trust *him*. And—and you know what, to some degree, I don't trust you, if I'm being totally honest."

She felt as if he'd slapped her. "Wow."

"You want the truth, right?"

"Yes, I do."

"Then there it is. We're in the waiting period, and before you ask me how long it'll last, I don't know. It lasts until I'm confident that you won't play me. That you won't change from the sweet, funny, cake-baking girlfriend I have right now into someone with an ulterior motive, who I no longer want to be with."

"Do you even know what love is? You're so afraid of being hurt—"

"I'm not afraid of being hurt."

"You *are*, but you won't accept the reality of those feelings. You're afraid of being hurt and afraid of being used."

"Because that's what people do, Lorna! It's not crazy to be cautious."

Her shoulders dropped in frustration. They were simply too different.

"I feel sorry for you," she said quietly.

His face hardened in a rejection of her words.

"You have no idea what you're missing out on. I understand why you're afraid. Love *is* scary. But it's beautiful too. I told you that my fiancé died, but I didn't tell you the whole story. I lost Marcus the night before our wedding, and I didn't know it. We agreed not to see each other the night before the wedding—sticking to silly tradition because we were worried about bad luck. Hah."

She broke off, swallowing hard. "He didn't show up to the ceremony, and everyone thought he'd stood me up, but I knew better. Marcus would never do that. He loved me. I begged his brother to go to his apartment and check on him. He and the best man left, and they found Marcus beside his car in the parking lot, in a pool of blood. He'd been attacked on his way into his apartment. He lived in an end unit, so his body lay on the ground, unnoticed, all night."

"Geez, Lorna, I'm sorry," Reginald said in a low voice.

"I was devastated. Not only for me, but for him. He was kind and generous and didn't deserve to die like that. Someone had killed the man I loved. The person I was supposed to spend the rest of my life with. It gutted me. I couldn't sleep. I couldn't eat. I hated the thought of him lying there on the ground, discarded by some monster who snatched away the best thing that had ever happened to me. The best son. The best brother. The best friend. The best future father."

She rubbed a fist across her wet cheeks. Though she'd lost Marcus years ago, talking about him brought back the pain. Her throat hurt from the sorrow of his untimely death. They found and prosecuted the person who killed him, but for her and his family, it hadn't been enough.

"I thought I'd never love again. Why bother? There was no one else like Marcus, and it hurt so much to love someone and then lose them for good. But then I decided to enjoy the beauty of our relationship. The good times and the laughter. Being loved by him helped mold me into the woman I am today. Loving him made me stronger and kinder. I hate that he was murdered, but I don't regret loving him. The pain I feel means that I was alive and able to experience something a lot of people never get to experience, and for that I'll forever be grateful.

"I really do feel sorry for you, Reggie. You don't know what that's like to just be free to love without reservations, and you may never know. I hope someday you'll find someone who can change your mind. Someone who'll make you eager and crazy enough to act outside of your character. Clearly, I'm not that person."

His brows lowered and his green eyes flashed with anger. "What are you saying? Is this your way of giving me an ultimatum?"

"Of course not. You don't do well with ultimatums, right?" She picked up her purse and stalked toward the door.

"Lorna, you walk through that door and we're done!"

She swung to face him. "You don't like getting ultimatums but you don't mind giving them, do you?" She continued to the door.

"Lorna!"

Her name was a raw sound on his tongue. Tears blurred her vision, but she kept moving until she was out the door.

There was so much more she could have said. She could have told him that he was the one man who had made her believe she could have a second shot at lifelong happiness. She didn't, because he wouldn't want to hear those words. Fear kept him locked behind an invisible wall, screening him from the danger of having his heart broken.

She understood. The pain of loving and losing could be catastrophic emotionally. But the pain of loving and winning brought immeasurable bliss. She only wished he would take the chance and play the odds and hope for bliss, instead of believing only pain waited around the corner.

Other than calling her name, Reginald didn't try to stop her, and that—more than anything—confirmed he wasn't ready.

Lorna dried her eyes in her car and pulled out of his driveway. She'd had her heart broken twice in a lifetime, but she wasn't giving up. Her man was out there.

They just needed to find each other.

20

"What's wrong with me?"

In her dark bedroom, Lorna sniffled, sitting with her knees drawn up to her chin and the phone to her ear.

"Nothing is wrong with you," Glory said in a firm voice. "Reggie is a fool if he doesn't see how wonderful you are. He's missing out. Not you."

"Doesn't feel like it. It's been four days, and he hasn't called. I miss him like crazy. I want to call him."

"Don't you dare!"

"I shouldn't have asked him anything. Why did I create a problem where there wasn't one?" She'd been beating herself up for days over her decision.

"You didn't create a problem. You asked him where you stood, which is a perfectly reasonable question. People are always saying communication is important in a relationship. Well, you communicated, and he communicated. You both found out where you stood."

"But now I'm alone, and I feel like crap." Lorna dabbed at her eyes with a tissue.

"You want my advice? Forget about him. He said he loves you, but if he did, he would have called by now. That's the hard truth, Lorna. Your instinct not to get involved with him was right in the beginning. You are two very different people who don't see eye to eye on your relationship status."

Lorna was reluctant to admit her sister was right. "Did you know he changed his off day to Mondays so we could spend time together?"

"Sounds like the kind of man who knows how to woo a woman in the beginning. Men are good about winning you over, but they're terrible at maintaining that pace. What you need to do is forget about him and find someone else," Glory advised.

"I can't. I—I'm in love with him. I want *him*."

"Oh, Lorna." Sadness filled her sister's voice.

"I know, it's dumb, right?"

"No. You just have a big heart and have so much to offer. Not every man is going to appreciate you, and you have to find the right one. The right one is not a man known for running through women, whose nickname was the Green-Eyed Bandit, for goodness' sake."

Lorna laughed and swiped a lone tear that escaped her eyes. "I should have never told you that."

"Girl, I knew he was trouble when you said it."

They both laughed and then fell silent.

Lorna sniffed. "You know what, you're right. I need to date and date a lot. To get him off my mind and out of my system."

"Exactly!" Glory said with enthusiastic approval.

"And I know where to start."

REGINALD TOOK his tray of food and sat across from Chase at the sandwich shop where they were meeting for lunch.

"Sorry I'm late. I got a late start."

Chase dabbed the corner of his mouth as he chewed. "No problem. I haven't been here that long. I got caught in traffic too."

"Days like this, I seriously think about moving to another city. Atlanta traffic is getting worse."

"Yeah, it's bad." Chase studied him with a deep frown. "What the hell is wrong with you? You look like shit."

"I haven't been sleeping well the past few nights," Reginald mumbled.

He was sleep-deprived and moving through life like a zombie. He hadn't shaved in days, and ever since Lorna walked out, he'd had a hard time getting out of bed. The other day he sat at a stop sign lost in thought, wondering where she was and what she was doing. A driver's angry car horn finally jolted him from his melancholy, and he pulled off.

Pride wouldn't let him call her. He'd told her if she walked out they were done, and she'd walked out anyway.

He and Chase caught up for a few minutes, discussing a party Reginald had thrown for a recently divorced millionaire who posted photos of his antics on social media for his ex-wife to see. Then they touched on the property management company Chase worked at with Wynter.

"So that's working out, with the two of you being involved and working together?"

Chase nodded. "Wyn and I have always worked well together, which is one of the reasons why she's afraid for us to take our relationship to the next level. She's worried that if we date and it doesn't work out, it could ruin our friendship and our working relationship."

"She's right," Reggie said, in a matter-of-fact tone.

"She's coming around though. Well... at least she was." Chase scrubbed his hands down his face. "Marcella is becoming a problem."

Chase had mentioned her in the past. Marcella was an employee who occasionally flirted with him despite his warnings to back off. The only reason he hadn't fired her yet was because she was one of the best project managers they had.

"Let me guess, she flirted with you in front of Wynter," Reggie said.

"You got it." Chase shook his head. "What about you? How are things with you and Lorna?"

Reginald grimaced. "Not good. We haven't talked in five days."

Chase's eyebrows snapped together. "What happened?"

"We had a fight, and she basically broke up with me."

"You're kidding."

Reginald set down his sandwich and sighed. "It's complicated."

"Uncomplicate it for me."

Reginald took a sip of his iced tea as he rearranged his thoughts.

"With Bria, I wasn't ready to be anyone's husband. I needed to get my business off the ground. I got it off the ground and thriving. Then I wanted to be a good provider. As far as I'm concerned, that doesn't mean only making money. I needed to save for the future. So I made sure I put away a percentage of my income every month for a rainy day. Business, set. Savings, set. Then I had to buy a house. The American dream, right? I've achieved everything I wanted to accomplish, and my life and finances are where I want them to be. I have a house, and I'm ready to be the type of husband any woman would be happy to have.

"Then Lorna comes along, and I think she's the right woman. Our relationship is thriving, and then, if you can believe it, I have the strangest dream. In the dream, Lorna placed a pillow over my face and tried to kill me."

Chase's mouth fell open and then he burst out laughing. "What?"

"I know, it's crazy. She's probably one of the sweetest people I've ever met, but that's what she did. I can't lie, it freaked me out. What do you think it means?"

"I'm not a dream interpreter, but it can't be good, that's for sure. Are you saying you broke up with her because of a dream?"

"*She* broke up with *me*, but I can't deny the dream was at the back of my mind when our argument escalated. We went to a party at her boss's house."

He gave Chase a rundown of what happened at the event and after.

When he finished, his cousin shook his head slowly.

"Why are you shaking your head?" Reginald asked.

"I knew you would do this."

"Do what?"

"What you always do. Run. We didn't even get to meet her."

"I'm not running. I just no longer think Lorna and I are compatible, and that dream was an omen. My subconscious letting me know I was making a mistake."

"Or, it's your subconscious sabotaging your relationship. Ever since Bria, whenever a woman gets too close, you find an excuse to break things off."

"That's absolutely not true." Reginald took a bigger swig of iced tea.

"What was wrong with Renee? You two were together for over a year."

Reginald shrugged. "She became too clingy. She wanted to spend every free minute with me."

Chase smirked, silently judging. "What about the dancer— what was her name?"

"Jocelyn?"

"Yes, Jocelyn."

"Three months in, she said she was in love with me. She was in love with the idea of being in love."

Chase pinched his nose. "Are you listening to yourself? You thought Renee was too clingy for wanting to spend her free time with you, yet you're spending every minute of your free time with Lorna. Hell, you changed your day off to coincide with hers. Oh, and Jocelyn was a problem because she told you she loved you after three months? You've been Lorna what— two months now? If your crappy appearance is any indication, I'd say you're in love."

"Do I look that bad?"

"Yes, you do."

Reginald rubbed a hand across his bristled jaw.

"I could go down the list of women you've dated, and for each and every one you'll have some crazy reason for breaking up with them. Though I have to say that breaking up with Lorna because of a dream is a new one."

"That's not why we broke up. She walked out of my house after making ridiculous accusations about my views on love. I can't get her to admit that old boy—her so-called friend—is in love with her, but *I'm* the problem?" Reginald leaned across the table. "By the way, in the dream, she was *suffocating* me."

They both stared at each other.

Reginald sat back and rested his hands on his thighs. Everything suddenly became clear to him. "I had that dream right after she brought up kids when we were at the Grady Baby Race. The crazy thing is, I had been thinking about having kids with her before that."

"But when she brought it up, it was a problem. You felt like she was suffocating you. Why though?" Chase asked.

"Because I want to control the pace of the relationship." Reginald let out a self-deprecating laugh. "I keep looking for reasons why she and I can't work, but the truth is, we're compatible in so many ways. Hell, we both can barely cook, but she can bake her ass off though."

"I remember you said she likes to bake."

"She makes the best pineapple upside down cake. It rivals my grandmother's."

"Maybe I'll get to taste it one day when you bring her to Sunday dinner," Chase said, with a suggestive arch of one eyebrow.

"If she'll take me back." Reginald stared at his sandwich in dismay. "I gotta fix this, Chase. I need her back. She's exactly the kind of woman I want. Funny, sweet, supportive. You should have seen her cheering me on at the race. I messed up, but I'm going to fix it. I don't care about Eric. If she says they're friends, then I have to accept they're friends. I'm going to get her back."

Chase smiled his approval. "Good luck."

21

B locked.
Reginald tossed his phone onto the sofa and paced the floor.

After two days of not answering the phone, Lorna had blocked his number again. That didn't leave him much choice to get in touch with her. He could stalk the coffee shop like he did before, but last time it took two weeks to run into her. He didn't want to wait that long to see her and apologize.

Maybe he could go to her job? No, Tessa had been kind to him at her house, but her close relationship with Lorna might cause her to have him forcibly removed from the property.

He could go to her apartment. *Yes.* He would go to her apartment and bang on the door until she answered.

Grabbing his phone and keys, Reginald left the house and hopped into his Jaguar.

After Chase had called him out the other day, he shaved and took over-the-counter sleep medication two nights in a row. He felt refreshed and looked like his old self.

On the way to Lorna's, he rehearsed everything he would say. It would take time to win her over, but he was confident he could do it. He simply had to put in the work, and she was worth it.

With a squeal of tires, he pulled into a parking space outside her apartment complex. He spotted her car near the building and relief flooded through him. Good. She was home.

Pumped on adrenaline and positive thinking, Reginald hurried into the building and took the elevator to the fifth floor. He had only been to her apartment a few times because they usually lounged at his house, but he remembered the number and that it was at the end of the hall.

He knocked on the door and waited.

No answer.

He knocked again.

No answer.

He knocked again and again, banging louder each time. "Lorna, open the door. I know you're in there. I saw your car outside. I want to talk and apologize."

He knocked again.

The door behind him swung open, and a shirtless fortyish-looking Black man with a graying beard stood in the doorway.

"Hey, buddy," he said in a gravelly voice, "she's not there, so please stop banging on the door."

"Where is she?" Reginald demanded.

"How the hell should I know? When I saw her earlier, she was all dressed up and left with some guy. Guess you're too late with that apology." He smirked.

Reginald's world tilted off kilter, and his heart tanked. "Was he wearing glasses?"

"Yes."

Eric McBride.

"How long ago did you see them together?"

The guy shrugged. "An hour. Two hours." His face turned sympathetic. "If you want, I can give her a message for you."

"No, that's okay. Thanks." With much less pep in his step, Reginald headed back the way he'd come.

"Good luck. Lorna is always bringing me a slice of cake, muffins, or whatever she baked. She's a real sweetheart."

Reginald paused. "Yeah, she is."

He dragged to his car and sat in the parking lot staring out the windshield, tapping his fingers on the steering wheel.

Eric McBride.

No doubt as soon as she told her so-called friend their relationship had ended, he made his move. Time for them to have a few words.

He remembered Lorna telling him once that Eric lived in an apartment above his business. With a quick Internet search, he found McBride Photography Studio, and within thirty minutes he was pulling up outside. The building below was dark because it was closed, but the lights were on in the apartment above.

That surprised him. He figured Eric and Lorna would be out to dinner or doing something else. Instead, they were up there together.

His breath caught. That motherfu—

Infuriated and boiling over with jealousy, Reginald exited the Jaguar and slammed the door. He leaped up the stairs that led from the ground to the apartment above. He pounded on the metal door and would figure out a way to break it down if Eric didn't hurry up.

Eric opened the door and frowned at him. "What are you doing here banging on my door?"

"Where is she?" Reginald pushed his way in.

"Who?" Eric shut the door and faced him with a frown of confusion.

"Lorna. Don't play dumb."

"Lorna isn't here."

"Her neighbor said she left with you."

"Well, she didn't."

Not believing him, Reginald searched the space, and his eyes landed on two empty wine glasses on the cocktail table.

"You typically drink out of two glasses at the same time?" he demanded, pointing. "I'm ripping this place apart if she doesn't come out now. Lorna!"

"What is the matter with you?" Eric hissed. "I told you she's not—"

A woman came out of the back in a pair of shorts and a tank top. Definitely not Lorna, but just as beautiful with dark brown skin and a huge Afro framing her head like a halo.

Reginald's mouth fell open. "Drea?"

"Why were you hollering for Lorna?" she asked.

Eric walked over to stand beside her. "He thinks she's here. Remember I told you he thought she and I..."

"*Oh*, right."

Reginald stared at the two of them. "What's going on here?"

"Drea and I are together. After Lorna questioned me about my feelings for her—no doubt because of you—I admitted that I had feelings for Drea."

She smiled. "That's why he would pop by and take her to lunch sometimes. So he could see me." She took Eric's hand.

Holy crap. Reginald's jealousy had created a whole scenario in his head where Eric was the enemy, but by the smitten look on his face, he was completely enamored with Drea.

"So you really don't have feelings for Lorna," Reginald said.

"No, I don't. I love her—as a friend—and that's all. What we had is long over."

"She never told me about you and Drea," Reginald said.

Eric shot him a tight smile. "Because she's a real friend and knew that it was none of your business."

Reginald's shoulders slumped. He couldn't believe he had gotten everything so wrong. "I went by her apartment, and her neighbor said she left with a man wearing glasses. I assumed..."

"I'm not the only man in Atlanta who wears glasses," Eric said dryly.

Reginald fell back against the wall. "That means she's met someone already. I'm too late."

"Maybe not," Drea said.

Eric shot her a look.

"If you don't tell him, I will," she said.

"It's not our place," Eric told her.

Reginald pushed away from the wall. "Tell me what?"

"We know where she is," Drea said.

Eric sighed and lifted his eyes to the ceiling.

"Where is she?" Excitement made Reginald's heart speed up.

"She's on a *date*," Eric said.

"But wouldn't it be romantic if he busted up in there and declared his feelings for her?" Drea grinned with excitement.

"Yes, that would definitely be romantic," Reginald agreed.

Eric looked between them, obviously conflicted. "If you hurt my girl..." He let the warning trail off ominously.

"I promise, I will not hurt her. I'm in love with her," Reginald said.

"Oh, that's so beautiful," Drea sighed.

Eric mumbled something unintelligible, and Reginald waited anxiously for the information, not daring to breathe and risk Eric changing his mind.

"She always texts me about the men she's meeting up with and where, as a safety precaution. She did the same thing the first time she went out with you to that French restaurant. I'm sure you know women do that."

Reginald nodded. *Just give me the goddamn information*, he thought.

"She's with a guy named Sebastian. They matched on a dating app and went to a movie." He checked his watch. "They should be out by now. Then they were going to dinner at a restaurant near the gallery where you and I met."

"Soul Kitchen?" Reginald asked. That was his and Lorna's spot. She took another man there?

"No. There's an Italian place around the corner. Beppe's, or something like that. I can't remember the name. Anyway, they were going there after the movie. She suggested it because she and I ate there once before, and they have good food."

Reginald was relieved. "Thanks. I owe you. I owe you both."

He cast a grateful glance in Drea's direction, and she smiled encouragingly.

"Make sure you don't screw this up," Eric said. "Lorna's a sweetheart. She deserves to be treated special."

"You're right, she is, and I promise I'll treat her the way she deserves. Thanks again."

Reginald rushed out of the apartment and into the night.

22

For the first time in his life, fear consumed Reginald. And for the first time in his life, he was willing to risk it all—pain, suffering, unhappiness—believing against the odds that waiting wasn't the answer. Being sure wasn't the answer. Sometimes you meet your person and have to conquer fear with action. You had to take the leap.

He pulled open the door of Beppe's Cucina Italiana and scanned the crowded dining room.

"Hello sir, may help you?" a pleasant-voiced hostess asked.

"I'm looking for someone. Beautiful woman, golden skin, great smile, short hair. She's here with a man wearing glasses."

"Are you supposed to be joining their party?" the young woman asked with a hint of hesitation in her voice.

He probably looked like a wild person scanning the room, but he'd never been so anxious to interrupt a dinner in his life. Instead of answering the question, Reginald continued to scour the room, and then he saw them.

His throat muscles tightened with tension, and his palms became sweaty. He knew what the back of Lorna's head looked like. He'd seen it plenty of times as they spooned in his bed.

The man across the table from her was wearing glasses and smiling.

Envy ripped through him. He should be the one seated across from Lorna. How could he have been so foolish as to risk letting her slip through his fingers because he was scared?

"I see them," Reginald said, and took off across the room.

He walked right up to the table, and Sebastian stared at him. Lorna stopped talking mid-sentence, and her eyes widened.

"Reggie, what are you doing here?"

"You wouldn't take my calls. I went by your apartment, and you weren't home. I found out you were on a date." He stared at his competition.

Sebastian's eyebrows pulled together in consternation. "Who is this?"

"Um, this is my ex, and I'm wondering how he found us," Lorna said.

"Never mind how I found you. I'm here to apologize and tell you everything I should've said before I let you walk out of my house." Reginald hoped she could hear the sincerity in his voice.

Lorna shook her head. "It's too late."

"It's never too late. Not when you love someone."

"Really, bruh?" Sebastian stared at him in disbelief.

Reginald dropped to his haunches beside the table. "You want me to open up, well—here I am, opening up. Laying my cards on the table. Leaving my heart wide open for you to stomp all over. I love you, Lorna. I want to spend the rest of my life with you. I want to marry you and have a couple of kids and have you and our children cheering for me on the sidelines when I'm running races. I want to cook breakfast for you on the weekends, eat your delicious cakes, and I want us to go to the estate sales to find those music boxes you love because it means I get to spend time with you. I love you. I probably loved you back in college, but I let that snake Byron slip in and take you away from me. I'm not letting another man take you away from me."

She stared at him in shock. "This isn't the place to have this conversation."

"Then let's leave and talk in private."

"*She's on a date,*" Sebastian interjected, sounding aggravated.

Reginald ignored him and kept his attention on Lorna.

"I'm sorry, sweetheart. I'm sorry for fucking up the first time we had dinner together in Decatur. Maybe I was subconsciously pushing you away—I don't know. But I'm sorry for putting my foot in my mouth and saying all those horrible things about relationships. I'm sorry for not answering your questions more enthusiastically when you asked me about kids. I really do want two, maybe three. I'm sorry for acting like a jerk after your boss's party, and I'm sorry I let you walk out of my house and didn't stop you. Give me another chance, Lorna, and I promise I'll make everything—all of it—up to you."

"Reggie, sometimes we have to go with our gut," Lorna said gently. "Your gut told you that I was not the right person for you, and I have to respect that."

"I never said you weren't the right person for me," Reginald said.

"You didn't have to. I know that's how you feel, and I'm not angry."

"Then why did you block my phone number? Why won't you take my calls?"

"Because I need to protect my peace, Reggie. I need to listen to *my* gut, which is warning me that you and I won't work. We're too different. If I forgive you, there'll be another incident down the line."

"No relationship is perfect and without problems. We have to work through them. Are you telling me you and Marcus never argued?"

"Of course we did."

"But you still loved him, right? Give me a chance. Maybe you're the one running scared."

Her lips firmed. "No. Look, I enjoyed my time with you, but our relationship is over."

"I don't accept that," Reginald said.

A server walked up, his hands clasped together and his face apologetic. "Sir, can I get you a chair so you can join them at the table?"

"No," Lorna and Reginald said at the same time.

"*Okay.*" The server spun on his heel and walked away.

"Look how in sync we are." Reginald smiled at her.

The corners of her mouth inched into a smile, but then she shook her head. "You should leave. This is extremely awkward, and Sebastian doesn't deserve this."

He turned to her date. "I'm sorry Sebastian, but I'm in love with this woman, and your date is officially over. I'm not leaving here until I convince Lorna to accept my apology."

"If that's all you want, then yes, I accept your apology," Lorna said.

"Do you believe that I love you?"

"Reggie, please, don't do this. We had a great time, but it's over."

"Answer the question."

"Go home."

"No."

"Reggie—"

"Marry me!" he blurted.

Her eyes widened, and her mouth fell open. "What?"

Sebastian stood. "Bruh, what is wrong with you?"

Reginald continued to ignore him and spoke only to Lorna "You said it yourself, right? When you know, you know. I know."

"All of a sudden you know?" Her brow furrowed with doubt.

Reginald took her hand. So soft and more delicate than his.

"Not all of a sudden. I knew after our first date. I couldn't get you out of my mind, and that's why I had to see you again. It wasn't an accident for me to see you at the coffee shop. I went back there every day for two weeks, hoping to run into you again."

"I kinda figured that's what happened after the barista called you out." She bit her bottom lip, and her features softened.

"I couldn't stop thinking about you after our date. I had screwed up and needed to fix it. Lorna, I need you in my life. Permanently. You're my future. So... will you marry me?"

She took a shaky breath. "This is a lot to take in."

"I'm telling you the truth."

"Dude, do you mind?" Sebastian asked, sounding appalled.

"You're sure?" Lorna asked.

"I've never been more sure of anything in my life."

"And you're not going to miss your freedom, and worry about your money, be afraid—"

"You can have it all." Reginald looked deeply into her eyes because he did not want her to doubt the next words he said. "I don't care about any of that. Just give me your heart."

Lorna shook her head, but she broke into a teary-eyed smile. "Yes."

Reginald stood and pulled her into a lingering kiss. Diners at the surrounding tables erupted into cheers, and Lorna pulled back, ducking her head and blushing.

"This is some bullshit." Sebastian tossed his napkin on the table and stomped out.

Lorna looked after him. "Oh no, I feel terrible."

Reginald pulled her into a tighter hug. "He'll be okay."

Then he kissed her again.

EPILOGUE

"**L**et me sit down for a few minutes." Lorna laughed, wiping sweat from her brow as she dropped into a chair at the table reserved for her and Reginald at Club Masquerade.

She fanned her face as he took the seat across from her. She looked sexy as ever in a striped bodycon dress that showed off the heft of her breasts and the curves of her hips. They had once again gone dancing, enjoying the gourmet food and music at the popular night club.

"Don't tell me you can't hang," Reginald teased.

"I can hang, mister, but I need a break."

Lorna cut her eyes at him, and he laughed.

As they both sipped the club's popular pineapple and hibiscus cocktail, Cameron Bennett, the manager of the club, approached their table wearing a friendly smile. One third of a set of triplets, he and his siblings owned Club Masquerade, taking over from their parents and turning it into the Atlanta hotspot it was today. He was the reason the club served gourmet meals. Cameron loved to cook and had hired away a chef from a popular South Carolina restaurant to oversee their kitchen.

"How are you two doing tonight?" he asked.

"Having a great time as usual, and the food is excellent," Lorna replied.

"What she said," Reginald agreed.

"Good. That's what I like to hear." Cameron looked at Reginald. "Were you still interested in seeing the rooftop?"

Reginald's stomach tightened, but he remained calm as he turned to Lorna. "Do you mind? They have a rooftop area that can be rented out, and it has a great view. I want to check it out because it might be a good spot to throw a divorce party some time."

"A rooftop party sounds nice," she said.

"Let me show you the space," Cameron said.

As he took them up to the third floor via the escalator, he explained that the rooftop was one of their more popular spaces. Upstairs, the thumping music was a distant sound.

He led them to the exit door and stood back so they could go ahead of him. "Excuse me for a few minutes. I need to check on something, but I'll be right back."

"Okay, no problem," Reginald said. Everything was going according to plan.

They walked onto the rooftop, and with no other guests there, the sounds of the night greeted them. Lorna gazed up at the dark sky and turned in a circle to get a full view of the space.

Soft lighting created an intimate atmosphere. The furniture was arranged to encourage conversation, with wicker sofas and armchairs filled with colorful cushions assembled around low tables and portable fire pits.

"This is nice," she breathed.

He stared at her, unable to believe his good fortune.

"What's over here?" Reginald asked.

She followed him, weaving through the furniture, and pulling up short when she saw a cleared out area with rose petals on the ground in the shape of a giant heart.

She gasped. "Reggie, what is this?"

He gave her a smile. "A proper proposal."

Taking her soft hand, he led her into the center of the petals. Still holding on to her, Reginald went down on one knee. As he did, Eric came toward them, dressed in all black and carrying his camera. Lorna's mouth fell open, clearly shocked they had worked together to plan this surprise. They had become good friends in recent weeks.

Reginald gazed up at her in the dim light. "I know you've already said yes to spending forever with me, but I'm asking you again. I want to give you everything you deserve and more —starting now—with a better proposal than the rushed, impulsive question I asked at Beppe's. I don't want there to be any doubt that I meant it when I asked you to marry me then. So I'm asking again. Lorna, would you do me the honor of becoming my wife, and allow me the privilege of becoming your husband?"

Her eyes misted over. "You're incredible, Reggie. Yes. A thousand times yes."

He slipped the emerald-cut diamond on her finger and then rose to his feet.

She tilted back her head, and he gave her a gentle kiss. Her lips softened beneath his, and she sighed.

Cupping his face, she gazed into his eyes. "You didn't have to do this, but thank you. I'll remember this moment forever."

"You won't have to rely on memory." He glanced at Eric, who took photos as he slowly circled them.

"Let me see the ring," Eric said.

Lorna extended her hand and happily displayed the brilliant diamond on her finger.

Eric snapped a few photos in quick succession.

"I'm so glad my two favorite guys are getting along now." Lorna wrapped her arms around Reginald's torso.

He grinned down at her. "Thank you for giving me another chance," he said.

"I didn't have a choice. Despite our missteps, I believed you were the right man for me. I can't wait to spend the rest of my life with you."

Reginald bent his head, and they kissed again, the sounds of the clicking camera capturing their special moment.

IRRESISTIBLE HUSBAND SERIES

More from the Irresisitble Husband series!

Read about Reginald's cousins and their path to happily ever after.

KISS ME by Sharon C. Cooper

He's in love with his best friend, but she doesn't believe in happily ever afters...

CHOOSE ME by Sheryl Lister

He's making his case for love...one kiss at a time.

Read the first books in the Irresistible Husband series and learn more about Axel, his friends, and how they find love.

LOVE ME by Delaney Diamond

Axel Becker believes Naphressa is the woman he needs, but convincing her they belong together will be a lot harder than he expected.

SHOW ME by Sharon C. Cooper

Just when he thought finding a wife was out of his reach...

DO ME by Sheryl Lister

She just might be his perfect match...if she'd only let him into her heart.

∽

Audiobook samples and free short stories available at www.delaneydiamond.com.

More black romance by Delaney Diamond

The Brooks Family series. Start with *A Passionate Love*, where nightclub owner Cameron Bennett meets and falls for heiress Simone Brooks. Will her wealth and status drive a wedge between them?

The Johnson Family series. Start with *Unforgettable*, where billionaire Ivy Johnson is stunned when her ex, author Lucas Baylor makes an appearance at her family's event in Seattle. She can't let him uncover her secret—that he has a daughter she never told him about.

ABOUT THE AUTHOR

Delaney Diamond is the USA Today Bestselling Author of sensual, passionate romance novels. Originally from the U.S. Virgin Islands, she now lives in Atlanta, Georgia. She reads romance novels, mysteries, thrillers, and a fair amount of nonfiction. When she's not busy reading or writing, she's in the kitchen trying out new recipes, dining at one of her favorite restaurants, or traveling to an interesting locale.

Enjoy free reads on her website. Join her mailing list to get sneak peeks, notices of sale prices, and find out about new releases.

Join her mailing list
www.delaneydiamond.com

facebook.com/DelaneyDiamond
instagram.com/delaneydiamondbooks
twitter.com/DelaneyDiamond
pinterest.com/delaneydiamond

CPSIA information can be obtained
at www.ICGtesting.com
Printed in the USA
BVHW020221280323
661268BV00019B/264